DIDN'T LOOK BACK

To Pat

enjoy the trip

Hubert Gilroy

"Didn't Look Back"
© 2009 by Herbert Gilroy

Published by Herbert Gilroy
P.O. Box 123
South Beach, Oregon 97366

Manufactured in the United States of America.

ISBN-13: 978-1-892076-67-0

Library of Congress Control Number: 2009936269

Gilroy, Herbert
"Didn't Look Back"
1. Title;
2. Northwest Author;
3. Fiction

First Edition
September 2009

How many times in my life
have I wished I could go back in time
just five seconds. But then,
I wouldn't have become
the person I am.

ABOUT THE AUTHOR

Herbert "Bert" Gilroy started working in a bowling alley setting pins at age eleven; he worked with his dad as a carpenter on weekends and summers until he was sixteen. He quit school and joined the Navy at seventeen – Bert and the Navy did not get along well. Two years later he was working at an automobile plant in Ohio, and from there, he went in search of the beats of the '50s, traveling all around the country, up and down the West Coast.

He was caught between the '50s Beat Generation and the Hippies of the '60s, and drugs and alcohol played a big part in his life for the next twenty years. In the early '70s he moved his family into the woods of Northern California and built a small cabin. That lasted two years, then fell apart. He worked in the logging mills in the woods of Northern California, and as a fisherman in the Gulf of Mexico; he worked as a fry cook and surveyor in Oregon.

In 1980, when he found AA and was able to stop drinking, he became a regular guy.

CONTENTS

● ✑ *About the Author* iv

● ✑ *Preface* v

1 ✑ New Orleans 1

2 ✑ The Scam 17

3 ✑ County Jail 35

4 ✑ The Fishing Port 53

5 ✑ Boys Town 63

6 ✑ Perfect Dawn 77

7 ✑ Meeting Old Friends 91

8 ✑ A Couple of Joints 99

9 ✑ The Storm 103

10 ✑ Vera Cruz 113

11 ✑ The Escape 127

12 ✑ California 145

Didn't Look Back

CHAPTER ONE

New Orleans

Around midnight the rain fell in a fine mist. I was pacing back and forth on a lonely stretch of road between Nashville and Memphis, Tennessee. Rain or no rain, the night was great; I felt like a free man. The rain was warm and you could feel spring coming on. I had hot red blood surging through my twenty-one year old body. I wanted to experience everything. I was free of my job, and the town I had left. I'd packed a few things into a small backpack and left. I had a restlessness in me and a thousand questions looking for answers.

God came into my mind again and again. I raised my arms to the heavens, the raindrops rolling off my face, my long dark hair soaked, water running down the back of my neck, and yelled out to God: "You and I have to part; I can't stand the guilt anymore. The pain I feel over the little things, I can't take this shit anymore, it's over!" I thought about that for a minute, and a picture of myself yelling off into the dark night to an unknown God, stomping back and forth, came to mind. I found it hilarious and started laughing like hell. Being on the road made my spirit soar; there was a newness in the air, like great things were about to happen.

ᥱᦁ

It was 1960, my twenty-first year on the planet and I had left Ohio twenty-four hours ago. The situation there was impossible for me. I had worked at an automobile plant outside Cleveland. I stayed drunk pretty much of the time during the past year and a half.

Automobile plants are nothing but traps. They pay good money and you stay forever…a slave to your own vices. I had just turned twenty when I began working there.

They had us in an office for orientation, one level above the main floor. The office was a small building that seemed to be suspended in mid-air but actually sat on steel girders twenty feet in the air, a steep spiral staircase running up to it. The office was centralized, windows all around, you could look in any direction for three or four hundred feet. A blue haze hung ten feet off the main floor. Thirty-foot aisle ways squared off every seventy-five feet or so. Machines in straight lines, boxes of parts, steel stacked all around, forklifts running back and forth, overhead cranes lifting huge stacks of steel. Each machine had a man standing or sitting by it, pushing a button, stamping out the part – TOOM-uush, TOOM-uush – eight hours a day, every day.

They had me loading boxcars. The men who worked the loading docks had always been there, young men working quickly, older ones more slowly, but assuredly. It was the older ones I watched: balding, vacant eyed men, worn out by the time they were forty, but their lives were validated. No way did I want to become like them.

My dad had gotten me the job, so it was not like I could just quit. I had joined the Navy when I was seventeen and that had only lasted twenty months. The Navy and I parted company with a mutual agreement. They were cutting back on the forces, and I found away out. My dad said they fired me. I was trying to prove that I could hold down a job, besides I was broke and didn't have the guts to just walk out and leave. I had to live it out a day at a time until its inevitable end. So, I drank!

I had picked up a book by Jack Kerouac: On the Road. These guys were traveling all over the country; writing prose-poetry-painting, putting poetry to jazz. It all seemed alive to me. I don't know if I'd ever heard any jazz, or could write, but I was willing to learn. I felt as if I were dying in Ohio.

It ended abruptly. I passed out one night in the wrong place, a woman's boudoir. Actually, I didn't wake up; I was dragged out by a couple of cops. I had been drinking all day and I got the brilliant idea to rob a tavern over by the plant where I worked. The bar cashed all the payroll checks on Fridays.

It must have been around eight in the evening when I staggered into a tavern, looking for this friend of mine, Jerry, whom I thought should share this experience with me. The bar was five feet to my left when I came through the door. I sort of fell over to it, arms folded against the edge. I stood there trying to act like I hadn't had a drink all day. It worked. The bartender brought me the drink I ordered. A few old timers were sitting along the bar, a card table in the back with five guys playing. Three booths were along the opposite wall. I looked around for my friend Jerry. A girl in her late twenties was sitting at the first booth watching me. Betty was her name. She was a big girl, heavy, short dark hair, with too much makeup. Betty was almost an ornament in this tavern. She came in the morning and was still there at night. She didn't drink all the time, sometimes she just sat, waiting. All the action in Betty's life took place here. I had felt sorry for her in the past, the verbal abuse she took from the men. Once in a while a new person would come in and buy her a drink. Her eyes would light up and she would be off and running. Sometimes the guy would have enough money to go two or three days, but most of the time they were good for a night.

"Have you seen Jerry?" I slurred.

"No, but I see you've been at it all day," Betty said, walking up to the bar.

"Yeah, I'm about half shot, need a place to sleep," I said, pulling a cigarette out of my pocket.

"Have you got money?" Betty asked, striking a match and holding it to my cigarette.

"Sure," I said, reaching into my pocket and tossed a bunch of bills onto the bar.

"I'll try to get you a room next door," she said, as she picked up the money and left.

I was standing there, arms on the bar, nodding, when I felt this tug on my shirt. It was Betty pulling me towards the door. I turned, followed her out and down the street. The hotel was a couple of doors away. She told me to wait; she would see if the coast was clear. I leaned against the door. Finally, I saw her at the top of the stairs, motioning for me to come up.

I staggered up the stairs. At the top, I started to fall backward, but Betty grabbed me and led me down the hall to the room. Once inside I took off all my clothes and crawled into the bed.

"I'm going to take a shower," she announced, towel draped over her arm. I passed out.

⁓

I awoke a while later to see this old scarecrow-looking guy sitting next to me who might have escaped from someone's garden. Another old geezer, balding, skinny as a rail, white nightshirt, perched at the end of the bed, he looked like the archangel.

"Get up! Get up! I want you out this hotel, now!" the guy next to me kept saying. "This is not your room."

"Leave me alone," I said, as I turned over. I knew I was having a bad dream.

The next thing I knew, I was being held up by my armpits, a cop on each side, walking me down the hall. I didn't have a stitch on, but my pants had somehow gotten into my hands. Awake now, I tried desperately to get the pants on. I must have blacked out, because all I remember is waking in jail.

It was a large cubicle, thirty-by-thirty feet, with a twelve-foot ceiling. A small structure, eight feet high, sat in the center, with three cells facing east and three cells facing west. The locks on the cells quit working years ago, so you could walk around the little unit and visit other cells. The jail had been built in the 1850s; iron rings were still on the outer walls, about three feet off the floor, probably used for chains and manacles in the old days, I thought.

Five other men were there when I was brought in. I knew them all from the bars. For the next two weeks all we did was read magazines, do push-ups, talk about what we were going to do when we got out, and walk around the six cells.

One day they called out my name. As I stepped through the steel doorway, I saw my dad sitting against a table in the outer room. The room was gray and bare, except for the table. The jailer brought out a box with my stuff in it. I thanked him and turned to my dad. He was an inch taller then me, 5 feet, 11 inches, auburn hair, curly and combed straight back. Abundance and the good life were making him soft.

"Well, how did you like that experience?" he smiled, sitting back on the edge of the table.

"I made it," I said, putting the belt through the loops in my jeans.

"You know, they fired you, and your mother's real proud. She read about your little adventure in the papers," he said, trying to make me feel guilty.

"Well, there's not much I can do about that," I said, putting my wallet in the back pocket.

"You can go and see about getting the job back," he said.

"I don't even know if I want it…but I'll check it out. Right now I need a shower! Can we leave?" I asked, combing my hair back with my hands.

He stood up. "Let's go," he said, walking toward the door.

I never knew if he had left me there to clean up my act, or if he was just broke.

When I went to court, the judge said I was accused of breaking into a woman's room and trying to rape her. The judge, having had Betty before him several times, laughed and threw the charge out of court. I still wonder whether Betty paid for the room, or just went up there and found a room with the door open.

That was enough to get me out of town, hitchhiking south. I was heading for New Orleans to hear some jazz.

Ⳣ

There I was, on the open road at the end of April; the weather was warm and cloudy. The first night out it rained on and off, but I got rides. The second night out I was in Tennessee. It was four in the morning when I lay down by the road and slept, a fine mist still coming down, it felt wonderful...*I was free!*

I awoke a couple of hours later, wet and freezing, feeling not quite so free.

By the next evening I was in Louisiana. It had just turned dark when I got a ride. I jumped into this fairly new Buick. "Where ya going, boy?" the driver asked.

He was a big guy, over forty, and heavy with a southern drawl. A salesman, I thought. I could tell he had been drinking.

"New Orleans," I said.

"You're a long way from home, aren't ya boy?" He asked, turning the wheel with great effort as he drove back onto the road.

"I left Ohio two days ago, thought I would come down and take a look at New Orleans, then head out to California."

"Well, I'll help ya out a ways. There's a bottle under that seat there, take yourself a pull, if ya have a mind to," he said. His seat was back as far as it would go and the steering wheel still hit his belly.

I reached down and felt the bottle, lifted it and took a drink. It was hot going down. I lost my breath a second, and then caught it with a big breath. I felt tingly all over, face flushed.

He laughed, "That's white lightnin, son."

"Whew...smooth," was all I could say.

He and I relaxed after that, talked about the weather, Louisiana, Ohio. We had been driving awhile, when he said, "Reach down and grab me that bottle."

I bent over and got my hand on the bottle and as I started up I caught a blur through the windshield, then something big and black hit the window, and flew over the top of the car.

"What the hell was that?" I yelled! the bottle in one hand, the other braced on the dash. I looked behind us. It was pitch black out.

"That was just an ol' nigger," he said, with a big smile on his face.

"What?" my heart jumped in my throat. "Let me out of this car!" I screamed.

"Settle down boy, relax, that was just an ole black dog. I was just funning with ya," he laughed.

"Are you sure about that?" I asked as the fear drained away. That black object just couldn't have been that big, I thought. I relaxed a little, but I knew I was in another country.

A half hour later, I was back out pacing on the blacktop, still anxious after the last ride. Twenty cars passed me before an old pickup pulled over. I was on my way again.

The drone of the engine and the lights ahead made my eyes feel as if there was sand in them. I could not keep them open. I just kept nodding out.

"Well, you're going to have to make a decision here, lad. You can go up to Baton Rouge, another forty miles, then back down…or you can take this shortcut with me," the driver said.

"Shortcut…huh?" I looked around, nothing, just darkness all around.

"I'll be going about twenty miles, it's another twenty miles over to the highway then forty miles to New Orleans. So…what'll it be?" he asked.

Not wanting to leave the comfort of the pickup, I said, "OK, I'll try the shortcut."

The twenty miles sped by.

ℝ

The loneliness set in as I watched the lights of the pickup disappear. The darkness was thick around me. I could just make out the road, at least it was asphalt.

"That was a big fuckin' mistake!" I yelled into the darkness. "Now you're stuck in the middle of nowhere, all because you didn't want to get out of that pickup," I said to myself.

"Well, there's nothing for it. Just walk asshole." I started down the road. A million things were coming to my mind. The scare I had when the salesman hit that black thing. He hadn't felt bad even if it was a dog. I remembered riding with this kid back in Walled Lake, Michigan, where I grew up. A dog was walking along the road, well off the pavement but the kid swerved over and ran him down. I had felt sick to my stomach and never got into a car with him again. I often wonder, am I the only one who feels this way about cruelty. Maybe you just get more callous with age.

I'd been walking for a half hour or so, mulling things over. I was thinking about my brother, Johnny, who was in prison in Michigan. He had gotten two and a half to fifteen years while I was in the Navy. He was a wild kid, not a bad one. Johnny was only fifteen when he was sentenced. He broke out of a boy's vocational school in Lansing, Michigan. Stole a couple of cars getting back to Detroit which was sixty miles and got tagged for almost everything that happened on his way back. If I'd been there I could have gotten him a lawyer.

Then I heard it! Something snapped in the woods to the north of me. I stopped dead, the hair on my neck standing straight out. I stood listening… it moved again, this time breaking several branches. It was big, whatever it was. It stopped! I started moving down the road, in a westerly direction, the woods off to my right about fifty feet. As I moved, it moved. I started walking a little faster, and heard off to my right more branches breaking. My guts were tightening, my mouth had gone dry, I was off and running. I could see a light about a quarter of a mile ahead of me. I was making for the light. Whatever it was, it was staying with me. It sounded as big as a horse branches were breaking all over the place. I heard a dog barking in the distance, I ran faster, it moved faster. What the hell could it be? The barking grew louder. I was running as fast as I could. It was staying with me. Then all of the sudden it slowed and stopped. I didn't! The dogs were less of a threat than the unknown!

I ran up even with a light pole. A house was a hundred and fifty feet off the road. The dogs kept barking, but stayed their distance. The house was dark. I stayed within the light, what a friendly light. I wondered," What the hell could that have been? Where the hell was I, anyway?" I knew there were bayous all around New Orleans, but how far they extended out I wasn't sure. Could I be in the middle of a swamp?

Up to this point not a car had passed. In the next hour one car went by. I knew it was going to be a long night. The dogs had quieted down. My adrenaline rush left me quite tired. After a while I laid down and slept, knowing the light was my protection.

I awoke to a bright, sunny morning. It was around seven o'clock, the sky was clear blue. There were rolling hills all around, a misty green from the dew. Birds were singing. It was as if the earth had gotten a cure from the beastly effect of the night before. I felt great again! A pickup pulled to a stop with a boat and trailer in tow.

"Want a ride?" the driver asked.

"You bet I do," I said, as I opened the door and got in.

I was off to New Orleans.

❧

My excitement cooled after walking eighteen blocks across town. I couldn't help but notice the "White Only" signs. What the hell was I thinking about I wondered. I'd come down to New Orleans to hear music of the Negro, jazz, and folk music. I wanted to get involved, discover the Negro's soul.

I remembered a guy named Rickfield, a colored kid in the Navy with me in Virginia. We'd all dress in our white uniforms, three or four of us walking together on base. Once out the gate, Rickfield would fall back seven or eight feet. I'd walk back and say: "What's hap'nin', my man?" with a smile.

"Man, I can't walk with you peoples," he said.

"Why not, it's a free county," I said.

"Not for me, it's not a free country," he said.

"Oh bullshit," I said. I'd try to walk with him, just to show him we could.

"Man, don't do this. I was raised in North Carolina. I know how to act. These are mean peoples," he said.

Rickfield and I spent a year and a half together. The only times we went out as friends were in New York, Cuba and Puerto Rico.

As I made my way over toward the French Quarter, I was getting this uneasy feeling. I had less than twenty dollars. Maybe I should say fuck this place, and get the hell out, I thought. No, I said to myself, you have to see the French Quarter and hear some music while you're here. Maybe I can pick up a job, I started feeling a little better.

As I walk through the French Quarter, I noticed the balconies off the second stories they had wrought iron railings, that hung over the sidewalks. Tourists with cameras strolled the streets, lots of bars on Bourbon Street. A couple of carriages stood by, with their Negro coachmen standing next to their horses. The coachmen wore tall black hats and tuxedos as they toured the French Quarter.

I needed a place to stash my backpack, so I headed out toward Lake Pontchartrain, a forty-minute walk. I found a place up off the beach where I could sleep and stash the pack. Lake Pontchartrain is a big lake, twenty-four miles across. As I walked along the beach, I saw a Ferris wheel a half-mile west of me… carnival, a job possibility.

As I came up off the beach onto the carnival fairway, the merrymaking was underway. I walked along through the crowds, booths on either side of the runway, noticing the pretty women, but remaining focused on finding a job.

"Hey, young fellow, come over here."

I looked around to see this guy waving me over. He was a carnie all right…five-ten, husky, chubby face with a mustache and a cigar stub stuck in his teeth.

"You're a strong young man, I know," as he grabbed my arm, "You weigh about a hundred and seventy pounds or so. Take this hammer, hit that button, ring the bell, and you're a winner. Ya can't miss, boy. Let me feel that muscle," he said.

I leaned over, "Who do you have to see about a job?" I asked.

He stepped back a little, and looked at me, "Go down there (he pointed west) a couple hundred feet 'til you get to the fun house. There's a little alley on the side, go through there and around back. You'll see a big red trailer there it says 'office' over the door. Got that?" he asked.

"Yeah, I got it," I said, looking down the fairway.

"OK, ask for Mike. Tell him Pete sent ya," he said.

I was gone, heading for the fun house. I found the red trailer. The door was in four sections, the bottom section was closed, the top three quarters were opened and I knocked. A bald head appeared. The man must have been on a chair with wheels. I could hear the rollers.

"Yeah?" he asked.

"Pete sent me over, said you might have a job. I'm damn willin' to work."

"Ya are, huh? Well shit, I wish you'd been here this morning," he took the cigar out of his mouth and stared at me a moment.

I stood there hoping.

"I don't need anybody right now, but I'll tell ya what – you be here next Saturday morning at seven, and I'll put you to work. "How's that?"

That's six days away, I thought.

"OK, I'll be here! You won't need anybody in the meantime, huh?" I asked.

"No, I don't think so. Just be here on Saturday."

"OK, I will," I said.

I headed for town.

☙

Darkness had engulfed me by the time I got back to Bourbon Street. Rain had fallen earlier. The streets now glistened from the lights and the dampness. As I walked, loneliness set in. People were coming and going from bar to bar. I would stand in the doorway and listen to the music. My money was limited, so I would have to pick the right place. I felt like an outsider. I wanted the comfort of a small bar and a few people who knew each other. I wanted to belong just for the evening. Indecision played with my brain. I found a little store and bought six packs of cigarettes. If I were going to stay, I would need some smokes. I stuffed them into my jacket and went down to the tavern three doors away.

The room was long and narrow, the bar on my right as I came through the door. Two guys were sitting on stools a third of the way down. A girl sat at the end where the bar curved to the wall. I grabbed a stool half way down the bar and sat down. The bartender stood waiting. He was thin with sort of longish black hair, a peach fuzz mustache. His serious dark eyes peered over horn-rimmed glasses. He wore a light cotton turtleneck and black vest. He had obviously been reading.

"I think maybe I better have coffee," I said.

"Which do you want – regular or coon-ass?" he asked.

"Coon-ass, what the hell's that, coffee?"

"Yeah, it's the local coffee, Cajun, made with a blend of chicory," he said, "and strong as hell."

"I might as well try some," I said.

I looked over at the girl, she was smiling. She had straight honey-blonde hair to her shoulders, very little makeup around the eyes, the nose was almost big, but blended in with the thin lips nicely. She was in her mid-twenties, almost beautiful. She looked at the bartender, "Brad, let me have another one of these, will you?" she said.

I thought about the bartender's name, and maybe buying her one. My mind retorted, You got less than ten bucks, no women 'til you get a job.

"How is the work situation around here, Brad?" I asked the bartender.

"Pretty tight right now, the Mardi Gras just got over last month, the tourists are starting to show, but it will get better next month," he said.

I sipped the coffee, "Whoo-ee, you weren't kidding. This tastes like shit."

"Well, that stuff's been sitting awhile. You'll have to try it when it's fresh. I'll make a pot if you want. We don't sell a lot of coffee."

"That's alright, go ahead and fix the girl her drink. I'll just have a draft."

As he picked up a glass to fix her drink, I said, "You don't sound like you're from the South."

"No, I've been here about six months. I'm from San Francisco – I went to Berkeley for a couple of years, then decided to see the country. My sister lives here, so I pulled in to see her, and I'm still here. As soon as I get the bread, I'm heading back to The City."

"The City?" I asked.

"Yeah, San Francisco, man. There's only one City. That's where it's all hap'nin, man. You've never been to The City?"

I shook my head.

He gave the girl her drink. "Well, let me tell you man, if it's going to happen, it's going to happen in The City," he said.

"I just read a book by Kerouac, On the Road. He talks about the scene in San Francisco," I said, taking a smoke out of my pack.

"Yeah man, North Beach, Sausalito…I just got a letter from a friend in Berkeley. He says there was a demonstration on the House Un-American Activities Committee; you know, where they're trying to find a 'commie' under every rock."

I nodded my head, like I knew what he was talking about. I didn't have a clue.

"They're even talking about a free speech movement."

"Free speech?" I asked, looking at him.

"Yeah man – to be able to tell it like it is. You can't say 'fuck' except behind the barn, or in a group of men. Women aren't…"

"Hey, you boys watch that language. There's a woman in here."

I looked up the bar at the two guys sitting there. The first one looked at us as if we had said something about his mother. He was a big guy, blond hair, combed straight back, a little heavy. The other one was thinner, just as tall, but with dark hair. They were both in their twenties.

Brad moved up toward them. "Just talking, I was trying to make a point – let me get you guys another drink," he said wiping the bar.

"Well, one more, then we'll have to find some action." The man had a deep southern drawl.

As Brad walked toward me he winked, "See what I mean?"

"Yeah," I said, taking a sip of my beer.

"Where are you from, anyway?" he asked, grabbing two glasses.

I tapped the end of my cigarette on the bar, "I'm originally from Detroit, Michigan. You know, where they build the cars, except half the town is out of work. I got a job outside Cleveland working in a plant till a couple of weeks ago. I thought I'd head out to California and see what's hap'nin', by way of New Orleans, of course. I'm at a point now where I need a job," I said.

"Automobile plant huh, that sounds like a drag. I don't know if I'd want to work there," he said, while holding a whiskey bottle upside down, pouring into the glass.

"It's not so bad. Boring as hell, but when you need money, you gotta work some place," I said. "Besides, it's not that easy to get a job these days. With this recession going on, there are layoffs all over the place. When Kennedy gets elected, things'll change… work will open up all over."

"You think Kennedy will get elected, huh?" Brad asked, taking the two glasses up the bar to his customers.

"Hey! I feel it in my bones. If there's one thing I'm sure of, that's it. Big things are about to happen. Mark my words, Kennedy is going to be the next President," I said, lighting the smoke.

"Now, you don't really think they're going to elect that nigga lovin' catholic, do ya, boy?"

I looked up the bar – the big blond guy was doing the talking.

"Where do you get that at?" I asked.

"That's easy boy. They're not going to elect no Catholic. The Pope'll be running the country in no time at-tal, and everybody knows you northerners are nigga lovers," he said.

"Hell, man, I was up in Detroit a year ago sitting in this drive-in, and a carload of white guys came in. They wanted us to go out and help kick the shit out of all these colored people. That doesn't sound like 'nigga lovin' to me," I said, standing up and putting my foot on the rail, one arm on the bar, facing him.

"Well, that don't sound too bad to me. You gots to keep them niggas in line, but all those northerners keep comin' down here fuckin' with our niggas." He looked over at the girl and said: "Excuse my language, ma'm, but this kinda talk gets me bent out of shape." He looked back at me. "Most our niggas are good niggas down here. You give'em a half a watermelon, they's happy, but you put strange notions in their heads, they just get confused."

I just looked at him dumbfounded. The music started playing behind me. Somebody had put a dime in the jukebox. I knew I was being sucked into this, but I couldn't keep my mouth shut, "I'm having trouble here, how in hell did you ever come up with that? That's got to be some of the dumbest shit I ever heard," I said.

"It's time to dance," a whisper in my ear.

I looked behind me, the girl from the end of the bar stood there. I thought a second, then gave her a quick smile…"So, let's dance," I grabbed her arm and off we went. I'm not a good dancer, but I knew I was dealing with a losing battle. Those two guys were twice my size and I couldn't open their minds with a sledgehammer, so I made my retreat.

"My name is Pat. I didn't get yours," I said glancing back at the bar. They were still watching us.

"It's Mandy," she said.

"Well, Mandy, I want to thank you for that. The problem seemed to be growing all by itself.

She looked at me as if maybe I'd misplaced a few brain cells.

"Problem or no problem, when we go back, you pick up your beer and come to my end of the bar."

"OK, if you insist," I said, as I stepped on her foot.

The heat rose in my face, I mumbled an 'I'm sorry' and swung her around. Another minute and the music was over. We walked back to the bar. I went over and picked up my glass and started back.

"Hey boy, you got more to talk about? You sure had a lot to say a while ago."

I looked back at the blond doing the talking, "No suh, you mens have a good evening now, hope to see ya soon, ya hear."

They looked at me hard, wondering if they had been insulted again. The blond one finally said, "Reckon we'll go find some night life." They got up and strolled out.

I sat down next to Mandy and Brad came over, "I hope they don't come back for awhile," he said.

"Me too," I said. "I know better than that, but in the heat of an argument, I lose contact with the reality of the situation."

"I could see that. For a minute there I thought you'd have to go to it."

"No." I lit a cigarette. "Like I said, I know better. You can't talk to guys like that.

They know in their minds they're right. Ya know, I had this friend up in Cleveland, he was a colored guy. We were coming out of the plant and this guy calls him a 'fuckin nigger'. The fight was on. My friend beat the shit out of him. The guy just lay there with a broken nose, bleedin' all over the place. My friend starting walking away and the guy says 'you're still a nigger.' My friend stops, realizes then that all the beatin's in the world weren't going to change this guy's mind."

Brad leaned on the bar, "Sometimes you can't get out of it. Those guys were getting pretty hot. I could see the blond, his face getting red, then it got beet red. That's when I told Mandy to play some music. It was her idea to dance."

"Let me thank you again, Mandy. Brad, fix her another drink."

"Thank you, I'll take it. That little story you just told. What? Don't you think you can change a prejudiced mind?" she asked.

"Why do you think I argue so much? You don't really know me, but it seems as if I'm always in an argument over this prejudice stuff. I just go with my gut feeling. If the truth be known, I think you almost have to kill every-body over two, then figure a way to raise those kids without our influence."

She looked at me, "I don't know, but integration seems to me to be the only way. Colored people need to have equality in the job market, in pay, and every school in the country needs to be integrated, not just a few. All of them, that means private schools, too. If they don't want to do it, close 'em down, Fuck'em." she said, picking up her drink.

Brad set two glasses down and listened. I leaned back to look at Mandy. You don't hear too many women say, 'fuck'em unless they're really mad. I was beginning to like this girl. She thinks things out, where I just rush in and make an ass of myself.

"What do you think, Brad?" she asked.

I started to pull out some money; there sure wasn't much left.

Brad held up a hand indicating he would get these drinks and started wiping down the bar. "I'm from San Francisco," he smiled. "We see a lot of these southern boys there. They either don't talk about racism, queers, steers, and weirdo's or they do pretty well with it. Some downright surprise you. If they can't take the city, they just come on back to the south. But, they never forget The City.

Three people came in and sat at the bar, up the way from me. Brad moved toward them and said, "But, I'm in total agreement with you, Mandy."

"Me too," I said. "We'll just have to see what happens." I sipped the beer.

"Well, nothing happens unless ya make it happen," she said.

"Where you from, anyway?" I asked.

"Alaska," she said. "I was in L.A. for about a year, before I came down here with my boyfriend, Bobby."

"Oh, you have a boyfriend, huh?"

"Yeah, he's a musician. He plays the clarinet and piano. He'll be here in a half hour or so. They're going to do some jammin' in back. You should stick around and listen," she said, running her finger around the rim of the glass.

Two more people walked in and Brad went over to the wall, turned a knob and indirect lighting came on. The colored lights came on bright, then faded down to dim. There were seven or eight tables and a piano against the wall, opposite the bar.

"You talked me into it, I'll hang out awhile," I said.

We sat talking, mostly about her trip out from L.A. She and Bobby came down here to New Orleans to see some friends and play a little music, then on to Chicago where she would go to school and he would try to perform in one of the clubs. She kept saying how good Bobby was.

I looked up and saw this guy coming through the door carrying a guitar case. He had straight, long, blond hair to his shoulders. He wore a gray checked shirt, black vest, with Levis; he was thin, maybe five-foot-eight. He walked over to the piano, got a chair and sat down, took out the guitar and starting strumming softly.

I started to comment on his hair, then thought better of it, but it did cross my mind that he had a lot of balls to have hair that long, this far south. Hell, everybody knew he had to be a screwball from California. Once he started playing, you kind of overlooked the hair.

Within a half hour six guys were playing. They had strolled in one at a time and starting playing, except for the bass player. He brought his instrument in on a dolly, then unpacked it and stood next to his bass strumming on the strings. When he finally started playing it was like he'd been there all the time. There was even a guy beating on a conga drum with his hands. The piano player, I took him to be Bobby – was the only one with long hair. They were playing "Summertime" in a way I'd never heard it. The piano player was singing about being a "motherless child" in a real high voice.

Mandy looked over at me: "Can ya dig it!"

"Yeah, I dig it," I said.

I felt good sitting there…safe. I wasn't thinking of the beach I would be sleeping on, or the dollar and a half I had in my pocket. I felt like a bohemian. It was great.

❧

"What!" I said. "You told me to be here Saturday. You said you'd have a job for me."

"Well, I'm all full up now. I don't need anybody, try again later," the guy at the carnival told me.

I walked away thinking what a fool I had been, sitting around all week waiting for this job. I had prowled around looking for work, but not too hard. I lay around reading most of the time. I hadn't eaten in five days. It wasn't too bad when I thought I had a job coming up, but now I was starting to get hungry. Well, maybe I could talk somebody out of some food down the line. I headed for the French Quarter. Somewhere down there was a bridge connecting over to Algiers.

I passed through a farmers market. On the way through, I grabbed a couple of bananas; that helped the growling in my stomach.

Crossing the bridge I stopped at the highest point and looked back. You could see all of New Orleans from there. Ahead a half-mile was a crossroads, not much else. A hitchhiker was down there where I wanted to be. Damn! I thought. Well, maybe he'll have some food or money. I started walking in his direction.

CHAPTER TWO

The Scam

I often wondered what would have happened had I slept one more minute. The drone of the car was in my brain – my eyes snapped open. A car! I was up and running before I even thought. I jumped out of the weeds and onto the road, thumb out, as an old, blue Plymouth passed. It slowed a little, and then pulled over two hundred feet down the road. I stepped back under the tree where Dave eyed me sleepily.

I met Dave a day earlier on the west side of the Mississippi in Algiers, across from New Orleans. He was shorter than I first thought, about five-foot-four, a hundred and thirty-five pounds, brown hair parted on the left and combed over to the other side. He looked like any college kid, clothes neat and trim, dark pants and green plaid shirt. A small leather suitcase rested on the ground at his feet.

He told me he was hitchhiking down to Monterey, Mexico. His mother lived on a horse ranch there. He told me a lot of things about himself, too much in fact. I had started getting a little skeptical. I figured he had a short-man complex.

We made it up the coast a hundred miles or so, then nothing. The rides just quit. Around ten, we crawled into the weeds under a big tree and went to sleep.

❧

As I ran toward the dusty blue car, I looked back to see Dave come out from the brush and onto the road. Two men were in the front seat. I opened the back door on the passenger side.

"Hop on in, fella," the driver said. The man was a big beefy guy; two hundred and fifty pounds, arm over the seat looking back at me. He had blond hair, blue eyes, and a big smile. Everything about the guy was big. The thick fingers of the left hand on the steering wheel held a cigarette. He looked to be in his mid-thirties.

I stood there a second looking at him and the back of the curly-headed man next to him, and then I jumped in. The car was a shambles. It looked like they'd been sleeping and drinking in it for a week. I had to kick beer cans over just to get room for my feet.

"I have a friend coming," I said, as the door opened from the other side and Dave got in.

"OK. Everybody in? We're off to it," the driver said as he drove back onto the road.

"Where you boys headin'?" he asked, looking back.

"I'm headin' out to California," I said, "Just to see what the action is."

He looked back at me. "The action's where the heart is, boy. You make your own action."

I looked back, wondering.

Dave scooted forward and put his left arm on the front seat. "I'm going down to old Mexico. My Mother lives down there in Monterey."

"Monterey, huh, now that seems like a place to have some fun. By the way, I'm Jewel, and this here fella is my brother Harlin. We're kind of rambling up inta Texas. He's sick this morning we've been partying down in New Orleans. He lost those teeth of his, prob'ly flushed them down a toilet some place. He's not talking much about it."

These two looked as much like brothers as Mutt and Jeff. Jewel, at thirty-five or so, looked big and strong (you could tell he lifted weights somewhere along the line), while Harlin was probably forty-three and was hunched over like an old man. He had curly brown hair, cut close to the head, brown sad eyes, high bony cheeks, and of course, no teeth. He gave us a sick smile and a nod. You could tell he had been big at one time, but now he looked sixty, and he didn't have a gray hair on his head. He had on a brown shirt, buttoned at the top, brown slacks. He must have slept in them all week.

"He's full of shit, I know what happened to those teeth," Harlin said, as he reached under the seat.

For a minute I thought he had his teeth, but instead brought out a bottle of bourbon and took a long drink.

"You want a drink?" he asked me.

"No, not right now, I just woke up," I said, as my stomach growled. "If you have anything to eat, I could sure go for that?" I said, hoping.

"My name is Dave," Dave broke in, "and this here is Pat. We just met yesterday outside of New Orleans. He hasn't eaten anything except a couple bananas in the last few days."

"Is that the truth now? Well, we'll just have to fix that. There's a truck stop a few miles up the road, if memory serves me. I could use a bite myself," Jewel said.

"That would be great," I said. "Thanks a lot. Say, I couldn't bum you out of a smoke could I?" I asked.

"All I have are Camels and there's no thanks necessary, I've been there myself a time or two. We're headin' up Fort Worth way. Ol' Harlin here, wants to get home to see his wife, he's getting tired of hanging out with my ass."

Harlin had been crunched down in his seat, head against the window, trying to sleep.

"I jus' want'a go home," he almost whined. "We been runnin' all over the place ever since you got out of the joint. You keep this shit up and you'll have my ass back in jail. I'm getting too old for this shit. I jus' want'a go home!" he repeated.

"I'm taking ya there, Harlin, but we'll need money 'fore long," Jewel said, as he drove along thinking to himself, his face serious.

I looked over at Dave and shrugged my shoulders.

"So, you really been in the joint?" Dave asked.

It was the first time I'd ever heard the term 'joint.' I waited.

"Yeah, I got out of Huntsville two weeks ago. I been pickin' cotton, plowing fields, and saying 'yea suh boss' too long." Jewel said.

"Where's Huntsville?" I asked.

"That's Texas State Penitentiary," Dave said. "What were you in for?" he asked.

"Hangin paper. I just did four and a half years. 'Yea suh boss,' four and a half long years," Jewel said.

"What's hangin paper?" I asked, feeling stupid about this time.

"Forgery," Jewel said, "Seventy percent of people in prison are in for hangin' paper. It's the easy way to go – just sign a name and you're off; no guns, no yelling, just a name. Ol' Harlin here was in for ten years when he was younger. You remember that, don't ya Harlin?"

"Hell yeah, remember it well. That was ten years of my life." Harlin reached under the seat for the bottle and took a drink, whiskey running down the sides of his mouth.

"Tell them about that ol' mule you had and your love affair with her," Jewel said.

"Well podner, let me tell you 'bout ol' Betsy..." For the first time since I'd gotten in the car, Harlin looked half alive and gave a big toothless smile as he talked.

"She was a small mule, nice round hips. I'd get out there in the fields and harness her up, rub her ears a little and tell her how good she looked, then we'd start plowing. You know, the more we plowed, the better those hips looked, just swaying back and forth. I'd get out far enough from everybody, then I jus' couldn't help myself. I jus' start fuckin' that mule. I don't think she liked it at first, but then she just took to it, like a nigger takes to corn-pone."

With the vision of Harlin fuckin that mule in my mind, it was hard to quit laughing.

"That's bullshit if I ever heard any. You didn't really fuck that mule, did you?" I asked.

"Man, when you ain't had no women for years...you fuck anything. Now I'm here to tell ya, I loved that ol' mule, but they wouldn't let me have her when I left...there's some weird shit happens up in that joint, more stories than people. I could sit here all day and never run out!" Harlin said. "And I been out twelve years now. Got a woman and a small place, had a job till Jewel showed up. But, I'm going back home, even if I have to eat shit to do it. No more of that joint for me."

"We'll get ya back home. I got a plan, but first we got to eat. The café is just ahead," Jewel said.

಄

I jumped in the back seat, on the passenger side of the old Plymouth and lit a smoke that I'd bummed off Harlin. It felt great not being hungry. I think I could have eaten three more meals like that. Dave got in on the other side, Harlin followed and got back in the front seat. "Jewel said he'd be a few minutes, he had to run to the store next to the café," Harlin said.

"So, those were grits," I said to no one in particular. "When I ordered those eggs I thought I'd get potatoes, but the grits were all right. I just didn't know whether to put sugar on them or salt and pepper. At least I knew enough to stay away from that coon-ass coffee," I said, as I rolled down the window and flicked the ashes off my cigarette.

"I like syrup on them, mixed with eggs," Dave said, as he stepped back out of the car to use the window as a mirror to comb his hair. "I think Jewel wants to go down to old Mexico with me," he said getting back in to the car.

"I don't care where he goes as long as he gets me back up to Fort Worth. I sure don't want to see him go back to that joint either," Harlin said, feeling around under the seat for the bottle.

I saw Jewel out of the corner of my eye, as he came around a car. He was carrying a case of beer and a bag full of stuff. He opened the door and threw the beer into the front seat, between him and Harlin. He tossed me a pack of Pall Malls.

"Here, need a smoke?" he asked, as he started the car and headed out to the highway.

Harlin leaned over and started talking about Fort Worth.

☙

Three beers later, Jewel said, "I think what we should do is take Harlin up to Fort Worth then the three of us head down to old Mexico. "What do ya think, Pat?"

"Hell, I'm not going any place in particular, sounds good to me," I said. "It's just that I'm so broke, if it cost a nickel to shit, I'd have to vomit."

"Well that's the thing. I'm almost broke, too. I was talking to Dave back at the café. What we're thinking about is finding a place that looks like it'd be worth going in. You and Harlin'll stay in the car, while Dave and I go in and do the thing."

Dave looked at me with excitement in his eyes. I knew he didn't think I'd go for it.

"Sure, why not. I'm tired of being broke." I thought of my brother up in that Michigan prison. If I ended up in one, maybe he wouldn't feel so alone, like the black sheep of the family. When we were kids, I'd try and take care of him, but he would always go steal something, and get caught. I was a couple of years older and didn't get caught as often, so I think he resented that. I was also tired of this guilt feeling I had about not being there to take care of things when he got busted.

I leaned back in the seat, opened a beer, and let Louisiana pass by my window.

❧

"OK, that's the place," Jewel said, as he pulled off the road. "You guys stay with the car. We'll be back in a while. Come on Dave, let's go."

I watched as they went over an embankment on the far side of the road and disappeared.

"Why don't you crack me a beer, Harlin?" I said, as I lit a smoke. "Does he do this much?" I crouched down in the seat, trying to make myself invisible from the street.

"Hell man, Jewel would rather steal than eat. He's gotten better over the years though I kind a thought he'd do right this time. I don't know what made me think that." He got the bottle from under the seat, and took a sip, wondering…

"Maybe I'll take a hit off that now," I said.

He handed the bottle to me and I took a long drink then gave it back to him. I leaned back in the seat, feeling the warm glow all over my body.

I had just finished my second beer when both doors came open, Jewel and Dave got in quickly. They were both laughing, Jewel started the car and off we went. They kept telling each other how easy it had been.

"First we got the back window opened and Dave crawled in, then he came around and opened the back door. We both went through that place like a fine-tooth comb," Jewel said.

"All we got was seventy-three dollars and some change, but I really thought I'd find a gun," Dave said.

"A gun! What the fuck do you want with a gun?" I could feel my nerves starting to tingle.

"Things just get easier with a gun, that's all." Dave said.

"My ass! Especially people who don't know how to use 'em. People shoot people with guns. Since I met you, there's been nothing to indicate that you know anything about guns," I said,

"Well, I do," Dave said with a lame smile, as he scratched the back of his head.

"There'll be no guns," Jewel said flatly.

And that was that, we didn't say any more about it. We went down the road, laughing, drinking beer, and telling each other what a good time we'd have in old Mexico.

That Saturday, as we drove casually up to the Texas border, we robbed four more stores. Jewel had become fond of Dave because he was always eager to go, and he was small and wiry and could fit into small places. Jewel would pull up to a place and say, "You two stay with the car. Dave and me will do this." So Harlin and I would stay with the car.

Then we were in Texas!

"I have to start watchin' my ass here. We'll do one big thing then get the hell out of Texas," Jewel said.

The sun was high as we went through Beaumont, heading for Houston.

"How far is Houston?" I asked.

"About eighty miles or so; we'll stop up the way and get some beer and the makins for sandwiches," Jewel said.

✌

We'd been driving up and down streets for about twenty minutes; we were in the industrial part of Houston. It was around eight in the evening. City lights were on, but total darkness hadn't set in yet.

"I think we'll try that place there. We'll go find a bar and have a beer, and come back when it's good 'n dark," Jewel said as he pulled over to the curb, then made a U-turn and headed back towards town.

I looked over at the low sprawling building, the fine-cut grass, and thought, I'll have to go on this one, so I better get my head together. Jewel found a main drag and pulled out, heading east. The lights started to thin as we drove. He spotted a bar on the north side of the road and pulled in.

"Let's go have that beer," he said.

We all piled out and went into the bar. I wasn't paying a lot of attention when I walked through the front door; I bumped right into Jewel who had come to a complete stop. I looked around at the sea of dark faces. A colored bar!

"Follow me," Jewel whispered, and headed for the bar. I was right behind him.

"Hey podner, let us have four beers, will ya," Jewel said.

We all stood there trying to look inconspicuous. All conversation had stopped; the hostility was thick, the music played in the background.

The bartender gave us a long look, shrugged his shoulders and hauled out four beers.

There were twenty-five or thirty people in the bar, but who was counting. Jewel paid for the beers with a big smile, picked them up and walked to the nearest table. We followed and sat down. Some of the people started talking again, others stared at us. We drank our beers, not too quickly though, and then headed for the door.

Outside, Jewel said, "OK, we'll try another bar."

We piled back into the car and headed down the road toward the bright lights.

ↄ

"I thought for a minute there, we were going to have to give our souls to God, because those niggas were going to have our asses," Jewel laughed as we sat down, beers in hand.

I looked around as I sat down – this joint was lit up like a Christmas tree, naked light bulbs hung from the ceiling, colored lights behind the bar, sawdust on the floor. The bar ran the length of the room. Eight tables were up front and small dance floor in the back. Thirty people or so stomped around, talking loudly. Whiskey bottles half full sat on tables, men stood at the bar drinking as music roared from the juke box.

"I kind of like dark lounges myself; why all the bottles on the tables?" I asked.

"It's a state thing. They can't sell liquors in a bar, but you can bring your own bottle in and set it on the table," Jewel said.

"What's that do for the bar?" I asked.

"The bar sells ice. Ya step up to the bar, ask for a glass of ice, and ya can drink all night," he said. "Ya have to buy ice every time the glass is filled."

"OK, you two stay here. Dave and me'll do this thing," Jewel said. He downed his beer as he threw a twenty on the table.

"This'll hold ya till we get back." Jewel set his bottle on the table and said, "Let's go, Dave."

I watched them leave, feeling my surroundings. These Texans were having fun.

A couple of them were arguing in the back. I had heard that most Texans had a gun someplace. I sat there trying to look as if I was from Texas; I didn't feel like I was from Texas.

"Well, let's have another beer, Harlin," I said, "It looks like a long wait

I was finishing my fourth beer when Jewel came through the door, Dave close behind. I felt the apprehension drain out of me; it had been building for the last half hour.

"You guys been worrying about us?" Dave asked, as he sat down.

"No," I lied.

"We scored pretty good, got everything we need, I'll tell ya about it later," Jewel said. "Let's have a beer then get the hell out of here."

We headed south from Houston.

"Man, I'm good. Ain't that right Jewel, I told ya I was good, Dave said. Man, I can break into any place…we're partners, ain't that right, Jewel?"

"That's right, podner. I'll pull over in a bit and show ya what we got, then we'll get set up," Jewel said.

Dave was still pounding his breast, when Jewel turned off a side road and drove a half-mile, pulled over and got out. He went around to the back and opened the trunk.

"Come on back here," he called out.

We got out and walked back to where he was bent over. I looked at the stuff in the trunk; a board lay across the back with a typewriter on it. Jewel rolled a check into the typewriter. He looked at me. "Here, hold this." The trunk light was on and I held the flashlight on the check. Jewel typed in the date.

"What name do you want to use?" he asked.

"Patrick McElroy," I said. "That's all the I.D. that I have, I'll just change my name when I get to California."

"We'll make this one for twenty-six dollars, easy for the first one, then eighty-nine on the rest." He typed them out, one by one, and then ran them through the check protector, a machine that squeezes the company number onto the check.

"Just like downtown…not bad, huh?" he asked.

I took one of the checks and looked at it, "I can't tell the difference, I'll just fill up the gas tank with this one," I said, then stuck it in my wallet.

We all stood around him as Jewel typed out the rest of the checks. I wondered what we looked like, standing there in the dark, with our lights focusing on the trunk.

Jewel pulled up to a gas pump. I opened the door and got out. The gas station attendant came over and asked how much I wanted. He was a young guy, dark hair, thin, wearing Levis and t-shirt.

"Go ahead and fill her up," I said. "By the way, will you take a small check? I only worked two days this week."

"How small?" he asked, scratching the back of his head.

"Twenty-six dollars," I said, trying to hide my nervousness.

"Let's see the check," he said. "It looks OK. You got I.D.?"

"Sure." I pulled out my license from Ohio. "I haven't got a Texas license yet," I said.

"No problem, this'll work," he said.

That was the first check. I now had money in my jeans, the first time in weeks. Not a bad feeling.

და

The sky was clear and blue as we drove through a small town in southwestern Texas. The main street quiet at ten in the morning. We made one pass through town then pulled over to the curb, across from the city park.

"OK, cash three checks and call it good. We'll meet back here in an hour. I'm not going to hang out long, so pay attention to the time. Let's go," Jewel said.

Jewel and Harlin left together, Dave struck out on his own. I headed west walking casually down the street, looking in windows, taking my time. I decided to grab something to eat. I spotted a café down a side street and went in, sat down at the counter and ordered a bowl of split pea soup with a glass of milk. My stomach wasn't feeling too good. This must be getting my nerve up, I thought. I ate my food slowly, thinking of the task ahead. I guess it's now or never, I thought, then got up, paid the check and walked out the door.

Back on the main street I spotted a department store. I would go in and buy myself a pair of Levis. I walked up to the front of the building. There were two doors. The one I stood in front of, and one fifty feet to the west. I went in the nearest one and started looking around. The counters were large; six feet square with mountains of clothes on top. The aisles were more like pathways through the clothes. I had to step up on tiptoes to see over the piles. I finally found the Levis and looked at them carefully, stalling for time. The place smelled of mothballs. In the center of the room was a counter mounted on a platform. A woman sat behind it. She was in her fifties, hair graying, half glasses set on the bridge of her nose, its chain circled her neck

"May I help you?" she asked.

I put two pair of Levis on the counter. "I was wondering if you would cash a payroll check for me."

"How large is it?" she asked, shuffling some papers, not looking at me.

"Eighty nine dollars," I said.

"Well, let's see it," she said. She looked thoughtful for a second.

"I'll be right back," she said, getting off her stool, and disappearing into the back.

A few minutes passed. I was getting nervous about this time.

"I'll just be a minute," she called from the back.

She must've read my mind, I thought. A couple minutes more passed. I should get the hell out of here, I thought. This is taking too long.

"There he is! There he is!" she screamed from the back.

I took a step to my right. A cop was coming through the west door. I hesitated a second, then bolted for the east door. My heart pounded in my chest. A second cop was half way through the door when I got there. I put my shoulder down and kept going. I felt more than saw him go down. Then I was on the sidewalk. The corner was a hundred feet away. Five or six people were walking by. I crashed into a little old lady, stopped, said "Sorry," and caught a glimpse of the cop getting to his feet, gun in hand.

"Stop you bastard or I'll shoot!" he yelled.

I was at the corner. He's not going to shoot with these people here, I thought. I made for the alley a hundred and fifty feet away. I was running as fast as I could when I made my turn into the alley.

I heard the shot and felt a slight pain in the little finger of my right hand; more air than pain. I thought I had been running fast before, but now I was flying. I ran around a couple of buildings, down another alley, then over some steps. I looked up and saw a sign: POLICE.

"Oh shit!"

I ran to the next street, made a left, ran two more blocks and there was the car, a hundred feet ahead of me. I stopped at the car, grabbed the door handle – locked!

"Goddamn!" I yelled.

I tried the other doors – all locked.

"The goddamn doors are locked," I screamed, jumping up and down. Two thousand miles away from home, in a foreign land and no place to run; I wouldn't know where I was even if I'd had a map. "Well, fuck it, that's the way the cookie crumbles," I said aloud, pulled out a cigarette and sat down on the curb, lit the smoke, and waited for the cops to arrive.

It didn't take long. A minute and a half later the first car came racing around the corner, sirens screaming at a loud pitch. The wheels locked and came to a stop. I looked up from the asphalt to see the first cop running toward me, face as red as a beet.

"You son-of-a-bitch, how did you do that anyway?" as he grabbed my arm with both hands and threw me up onto the car, catching the back of my neck and smashing my head into the hood. "What do you think of that, funny guy!" he yelled into my ear.

By this time a second wailing car braked to a standstill; an older cop got out.

"Easy there, Bill," the older cop said. "We got to talk to this here rabbit. Take him on up to the jail. And then we'll have a little talk with this here boy." The first cop shoved me into the back seat and slammed the door of the car. They all wore light tan uniforms and large Texas hats. They looked big as hell.

☙

They had me in a small office, on the first floor of a three-story building. I sat in an office chair with rollers, three men surrounded me. They had already punched me in the head several times, and in the rib cage.

"Where's the rest of the gang?" one asked, standing tall over me.

"What gang? There's no gang," I said, my hands cuffed behind me.

My brain exploded as a fist came from nowhere and hit me in the temple.

Someone grabbed me around the throat, threw a knee into my groin. "You sorry son-of-a-bitch, I don't know how you outran that bullet. But you're not going to outrun this beating."

"Aw, Bill, let up on 'em. Yer just pissed that your bullet missed," I heard someone say behind me.

I looked up at Bill. He was six-two, late twenties. His raw, boney face was red, splotched from exerting himself.

"I didn't miss him. I hit exactly where I shot. The som'bitch turned when I fired. How could he be so lucky?"

"Well, we could let him go, and see if he could outrun a 'nuther bullet," a third whining voice said.

"Naw, we're not getting into that, these guys are wanted all over the state," the second voice said. "Jack, take this lucky fucker, and put him upstairs."

I hadn't seen the old guy standing just outside the door. "Can you walk all right, young fella?" he asked.

I stood up. Everything seemed to be in working order. "I think so," I said.

"Well, come along now," he said,

Jack was about sixty, tall, slim, hunched over at the shoulders, he wore the same uniform as the cops, but I figured he was the jailer. We walked down the hall to the elevator.

"You ever been in jail around here before?" he asked, pushing the button.

"No," I said, rubbing the side of my head, wondering if my nose was broke.

"It's 'Sir'."

I looked at him, to see if he was serious. He was. The elevator door opened and we stepped in.

"When you talk to me or anyone with a uniform, you say 'Sir'."

"Yes Sir." The doors closed and the uplift grabbed my stomach.

"That's better, he said. Now you take nice guys, that's me, but some of these people ain't so nice. Fact is, they can be pretty tough. You take Bill for instance; he's one of the best marksmen around, and you've embarrassed him. You're the one that got away. He won't forget it," the elevator doors opened.

"Thanks for the warning – Sir," I said, and meant it.

We stepped out into a long, gray room. A four foot high counter immediately to my right; a big iron door opposite the elevator.

"Here, let me get those cuffs off," Jack said, lifting the gate and moving behind the counter. Take all your personal stuff out of your pockets and put it up on the counter; the belt to."

"They took all my stuff. Downstairs," I said.

"I'll get that later," he said.

Jack finished booking me in, then opened the big iron door and we went through. A long corridor stretched out fifty feet, cells on either side. Cyclone fencing covered the bars. As I walked along, I couldn't see into the cells, until I was at a ninety-degree angle to them. Jack opened a cell door. To my surprise, Jewel stood there, in the middle of the room, looking at me, a smile on his face.

"In you go now. You missed lunch, I'll see if I can get you some coffee," Jack said.

The room was big, with more fencing on three sides. To the left were three cells, two bunks each, one on top of the other. Each cell had a sink and toilet. A shower and sink on the back wall; a concrete picnic table to the right. The big door banged closed.

"How the hell did you get here? I just took a beating downstairs. They were trying to find out who was with me. They kept asking where the gang was. The dirty bastards had you all the time."

Harlin was sitting on a bench at the picnic table, one leg crossed over the other, cigarette dangling from his fingers, staring at the floor. He looked like he had the blues, bad.

"Hell, Man, they had us in fifteen minutes of our splitting. What happened with you?" Jewel asked. "We heard about the shooting. Ol' Jack there has been keeping us up to date."

I sat down on the picnic table and began a rundown of the events which happened from the moment we split up. Jewel kept asking questions, and laughed like hell when I told him about knocking the cop down at the door, then running up to the police station.

"If they had you in fifteen minutes, they kicked the shit out of me for nothing better to do. They must have known I was out there. They just waited for me to show myself."

"That's it. Our little friend tried to buy a gun. They had him in five minutes. He started squealing like a pig going to slaughter. The rest is history," Jewel said.

"Where's Dave now?" I asked, taking out a cigarette and lighting it.

"He made up to the chief, somehow. They don't want him in here with us."

I heard the big door open. We waited. Jack appeared.

"McElroy…here's a cup of coffee, you'll have to wait till dinner to eat," Jack said.

"Hey thanks, I appreciate this – uh, sir."

"No thanks necessary. After that run this morning, you deserve it. Why, you boys are the biggest thing to happen here in years. The whole town's up and talking; they're even comparing you to the Daltons," Jack said.

"The Daltons, Why, they can't do that, can they? Two days ago, I was hitchhiking down the road, now they're comparing me to the Daltons. What kind of shit is that?" I said, setting the cup on the table. I had this nagging fear in my gut that maybe I stuck my foot in it this time.

Jewel stepped up to the cell door, grabbed onto a bar and said, "Jack, tell the boss man that I'm ready to talk to him."

"OK. But you're still big news." Jack walked back down the hall shaking his head until he was out of sight.

"What's that all about?" I asked, stepping up to the bars.

"I been doing some hard thinking on this, Jewel said. I have to get my brother out of this mess, so this is the plan. They're going to throw the bitch at me anyway you look at it. I'm going to cop to everything, me and Davey boy. That'll get you off the hook and I want you to clear Harlin. That'll leave you with the one check. I can't get you out of that one, boy."

"Hell, I don't know what to say, man. What's the 'bitch,' anyway?"

"Habitual criminal, it gets you fourteen years, automatically. I been trying to figure a way out of it, but I can't, and I have to get Harlin out of this, and back home."

"Habitual criminal, I never heard of it before," I said.

Jewel pulled out a cigarette, walked over to the table, sat on it, and lit the smoke. I took a drink of coffee and walked over to Jewel.

"You get busted three times, and that's it. They throw the bitch at you. That's the state of Texas for ya, and this is my time," he said.

"God, I hate to see you do all that time," Harlin piped up.

It's like Harlin had been in a trance and he suddenly snapped out of it. He had a pained look on his face, then bewilderment. He started wringing his hands. He stood up and paced back and forth along the bars.

"There's gotta be somethin' you can do." He kept pacing.

Lowering my voice, leaning over to Jewel, I said, "He could be having a nervous breakdown."

"Naw, he'll be all right. I'll have a talk with him." Jewel walked over and put his arm around Harlin's shoulder and started talking in a low, soothing voice.

I didn't know what I was talking about. After the shock of the morning was wearing off, I felt that I was having the nervous breakdown. I went over to a window on the back wall. There were bars over it. I could see a parking lot in the back of the jail, it was asphalt, with spaces painted in. I stared at the lot, wondering want kind of jam I had gotten myself into this time. I felt like crying, but knew that wouldn't get me out of this place. I grabbed the bars tight with both hands and pulled sideways with everything I had. The bars didn't move, but I felt better.

"Hey hombre, Que Paso?"

I looked around to see who was doing the talking. A Mexican was sitting on the other side of the bars, opposite the table.

"You talking to me?" I asked, looking through the fencing on the bars, I could see two men sitting on the floor, a set of dominoes between them. Beyond them, four white men sat playing cards at a table in the center of the room.

"Do you have a smoke? My family will be here this afternoon with some stuff, but I'm out for the time being," he said.

"Sure," I said, handing him a cigarette through the bars.

"You're the rabbit they took a shot at this morning, huh?" He sat cross-legged, Levis, white t-shirt, head cocked back, with a big smile on his pudgy face.

"Hell! Things happened so fast, I wasn't even sure they shot at me, till it was over. I must have turned at exactly the right moment," I said.

The iron door clanked open and the jailer appeared, "Madden, come on out here. They want to talk to you downstairs."

I looked around to see who he was talking to. Jewel stepped forward.

"I'll be back," he told Harlin and nodded to me on his way out. Harlin kept pacing along the bars. I stepped back to watch the domino game, still sipping coffee.

Two hours later the door clanked open and Jewel walked through it.

"That's it," he said. "Now it's up to the fates."

"So what happens now?" I asked.

"Nothing, this here is a holding tank. There are several holds on us. It'll be awhile before we get to court. They'll prob'ly run us around to a few jails, then they'll settle on one place. In the meantime, we play cards," He showed me a deck.

Two days passed. I was getting tired of watching the parking lot, playing cards and talking about nothing. Breakfast was handed through a little opening in the door. I was even sick of that.

"There'll be a Texas Ranger picking you up this morning, McElroy," Jack said, handing breakfast through the opening on the third day.

"Where's he taking me?" I asked, a little too quickly, fear scratching at my stomach.

"Don't know," he said dead-pan.

"You hear that, Jewel?" I asked, taking the toast and syrup over to the wall and sitting down next to the bars.

"Yeah, I heard. Those Texas Rangers are some mean sons-a-bitches," he said, chewing on a piece of toast.

"Well, I'm small potatoes," I said.

"I heard about this guy, they took him out in the desert, pulled his pants down, and tied a wire around his balls, then took the other end and stuck it to a battery. He told them what they wanted to know all right," Jewel said.

My nuts sort of retracted at the thought, a chill ran through me.

"There was this other time, they took a guy, put him in a potato bag, tied it off, then threw him off the bridge. They picked him up five hundred feet down river. He was like a drowned rat, screaming to tell them what they wanted to know. All I know is that they are meaner than junkyard dogs." He looked at me with those smiling blue eyes.

"Ha, ha, ha," I said, "OK. You got me scared shitless." I almost meant it.

"You'll be all right." He looked me in the eye and said, "You're tougher than you think, sport."

I almost believed him.

They picked me up at eleven a.m. I said goodbye to Jewel and Harlin and went out the door.

Didn't Look Back

CHAPTER THREE

County Jail

The solid steel door closed behind me. The small trapdoor in the center that food was slipped through was closed. The room before me was big and spacious. Most of these jails were about the same, this being my sixth in a week. Armed guards would take me to a jail; keep me a day or so, then on to the next one. I didn't have a clue as to where I was. I lost track after the third. I stood in the bullpen, as they called it. A small man, sat cross-legged at the table that ran lengthwise to the bars, playing solitaire. He was in his forties, receded brown hair, five-foot-four, hundred and thirty pounds. He wore a t-shirt with blue pants. He looked at me with cold, gray eyes and calmly went back to playing cards. A shower was to my left, against the wall. To my right was an aisle and a cell doorway; the door slid sideways into the wall. As I walked down the aisle, I noticed a curly head in the top bunk of the first cell. The two bottom bunks were down and made up in the second. On to the third cell where I looked in – the two bottom bunks were down with mattresses. The top two were unused and up against the wall to allow for more light. A Mexican lay on the one to my left; he sat up as I came in.

"Anybody using this bunk?" I asked, throwing my stuff down on the lower bunk.

"No, nobody's got it," he said, standing up and moving to the doorway.

He looked kind of funny standing there, dark eyes staring at me, his head shaved. He wore a pair of Levis no shirt, he was five nine, one hundred fifty pounds, with a visible rupture under each armpit. They looked like two base-balls just under the skin. He also had one in the center of his rib cage, and I would bet his nuts were ruptured too. I didn't ask.

The mattress was doubled up on my bunk. Grabbing it and throwing it out, I said, "My name is Pat. You don't mind a roommate, do ya?"

He shook his head, "No man, I could use the company."

They gave me a sheet and blanket when I came in. The sheet was like a pillowcase, the mattress went inside. After getting the mattress inside, I folded the blanket. The Mexican had stepped out into the walkway while I got my bunk straightened up. He came back in, sat down on his bunk, lighting a Marlboro cigarette. "You gonna be here a while?" he asked taking a deep drag on the smoke.

"I hope not. I should go to court pretty quick now if this is my last jail," I said, sitting down on the bunk, checking the firmness of my mattress.

"What you in for?" he asked.

"Bad checks," I said

"Well, that's a felony. You have to wait for the grand jury; that won't be till October."

"October! You mean I have to sit here till then? That's five months!" I sat down on the bunk, trying to think of a way out of here.

"You got a smoke?" I asked, "They confiscated all my money, all because of one check."

The Mexican got a pack of Marlboros from under his mattress and handed me one.

"Hopefully, they'll just kick me out of here. When's dinner – around five?"

"No, you missed it." He gave me a thick lipped smile, showing beautiful white teeth. He tossed a book of matches over to me.

"Damn! I missed lunch, no dinner, and you tell me I have to sit here till October. This is not a good day." I busted off the filter and lit the smoke. "Fuck it, that's the way it goes," I lay back on the bed, my head against the wall smoking.

A picture of a young girl, one of an older woman and a family group shot, on the wall next to him. A box of goodies with tin foil sticking out lay beside his cot.

"You look like you'll be here a while," I said.

"Yeah, I have a few felonies on me. I'll be here till October. My name is Tommy Garcia, and I have no money for bail."

"It looks like you have family out there?" I nodded toward the pictures.

"That's my mother, this is Consuela, she loves me very much," he sat there looking at the pictures. "My bail is too high," he said.

"Are you from around here?" I asked.

"Yeah, I've been in this town most of my life."

"What town is this anyway?"

"This is Benton. You're in the Benton County jail, amigo."

I stood up, took off the t-shirt I'd been wearing, and threw it on the bunk. I walked out to the bullpen, then over to the bars by the table.

"How's it going?" I said to the little guy playing solitaire.

He looked up at me, but said nothing.

There was a hallway on the other side of the bars, a big window in the wall that overlooked the courthouse across the street. I could see the cars parked along the far side of the street, and the main entrance to the courthouse. A large dome sat perched on top of the courthouse, a big clock embedded in the center of it. The street was quiet at this time of day. It was ten past three in the afternoon

"You play cards?" the little guy asked, putting a cigarette between his lips.

"Sure," I said. "You know, poker, crazy eight, solitaire, but I've never seen that kind of solitaire." I pointed to his cards, they were in a pyramid.

"There's all kinds of solitaire. How 'bout hearts, can you play that?"

"No, but I'm willing to learn. There doesn't seem to be much else to do."

"Tommy!" He yelled, "Come on out, we need a third player. Sit down, I'll give you a run down. By the way, my name is Bob."

I sat down as Bob dealt the cards. "I'm Pat."

"OK, Pat, you're looking for suits. The queen of spades is the bitch."

Keys rattled in the main door, it opened. A little guy, a hundred thirty pounds, skinny as a rail, walked into the room. His cheeks were red, like someone had just slapped his face. He had on light tan pants and a t-shirt. Hands in his pockets, head down, he walked back to the cells without looking at us.

"They had him down for questioning, I guess. He's been in the same cell with me for two days. Hasn't said a word, I think he's a little haywire, or just scared shitless," Bob said, then went about showing me a couple more hands of hearts. "I wonder where the hell Tommy is," Bob said.

"I'll see what's happening with him," I said. I got up and went to the back cell. There was Tommy, sitting on his haunches, arms wrapped around his knees. A fire was burning under a steel cup of coffee.

"What the hell you doing?" I asked, kneeling down beside him.

"Not so loud," he said, "I'm fixing coffee."

"I see that, but how the hell did you do that?"

"You just get toilet paper, wrap it around your hand real tight, fold it at the bottom so it bunches up in the center, then light it, it'll burn long and slow. Put a hook in the wire and hang it over the bar, make a circle in the other end, put the cup in and TA-DA, you're cookin'. Don't let your coffee cup go back in the morning, you need a cup to cook in.

Tommy reached down and grabbed the burning paper, flushed the toilet and dropped it in.

"All right," I said. "Let's play cards."

About an hour passed. I sat studying my cards, then looked up. There stood Harlin.

"Harlin! How long you been here?" I yelled.

He was wearing the same brown pants with a t-shirt. He stood there scratching his balls, yawning, wondering where he was. I wanted to go over and give him a big hug, but I didn't. Just seeing a familiar face made me feel better than I had all week. I lay the cards down. "I'll be back," I said, and walked over to Harlin.

"Where's Jewel?" I asked.

"They took him to Houston, that's the last I heard. It's hard being back in these jails. I talked to my sister the other day about the bail, its five hundred dollars. She told me she'd get it up in a few days, maybe a week," he pulled out a Pall Mall and lit it.

"Hey, can I get one of them?" I asked

Harlin handed me a cigarette. We walked over by the bars and he sat down at the table. I put my arms on the bars and looked out the window. The employees of the courthouse were getting off work. I stood there watching them flow out the door, going their separate ways. They would get in their cars and go home to children, family, get dinner on the table; make love to their mate. Envious feelings arose in me, I felt sad for a moment, but only a moment. I knew that if I were on the streets I wouldn't be going home to dinner. There's so much in life that I haven't done, that's why I'm in this situation. It's almost comical, so it can't be all that bad. The two-car garage, two point two kids, the white picked fence, and the little woman waiting at the door when I came home from the daily grind would have to wait.

"What about the kid? You know, Dave?" I asked Harlin.

I turned around to look at Harlin. Tommy had stood up and come over by the bars to watch the women as they left the courthouse. Bob had disappeared. Harlin sat there staring at the floor.

"They gonna put that dumb kid in some kind of school, I guess. Hell, I don't know," Harlin said

"Well, good for Dave," I said, feeling a distance between Harlin and myself. Jewel must have been the cohesive link.

"Chinga soo madra, I wanna get out of this place, did you see all those wim'in?" Tommy said, and began pacing.

"How you fellas doing?" A colored guy stood looking at us from outside the cell, in the hallway between the window and the bars. He wore a full length pair of white overalls, had close cropped hair, big eyes, high cheek bones, and a big smile. Chocolate silk is the only way I could describe his face. He sat down, legs crossed straight out in front of him, "I see a new face in there," he said.

"Yeah, I'm the new guy on the block, Pat's the name," I said.

"Heard bout you downstairs, yer the one gave those poo-lice a hard time over in Baker, outran the bullet. They didn't like that shit atall, you being a northern boy and all."

"You seem to know more about me than I know about myself," I said.

"The bennies of being a trustee, I get all the info. They call me Willie," he said.

"You got a smoke I could get, Willie?"

"Now this boy thinks cigarettes grow on trees. You got one this time, but I ain't your pappy, so don't spect me to raise ya." He handed me a smoke as he winked at Tommy.

Any other time I might have told him to stick it up his ass, but cigarettes had become a rare item.

"Thanks," I said.

I heard loud yelling behind us. It sounded like something hit the wall. Tommy ran for the back, I followed him through the doorway to the second cell. Bob was slamming the little guy up against the bars.

"You filthy fucker, I want you out of this cell, right now!" Bob pushed him out the door, went back in, grabbed the little guy's mattress and tossed it out onto the floor.

"What happened?" I asked.

"I don' know," Tommy said.

The little guy was pacing back and forth, on the far side of the bullpen, his arms folded, hands stuck into his armpits, shoulders up around his ears.

"If you ask me, I think he's about to blow," I said, walking back to the table.

"Woo-EE, I thought we were going to have a good one there for a minute; Bob was pissed off at something," Tommy said, sitting down at the table.

I joined him and started flipping through the books that were lying on the table, keeping an eye on the guy doing the pacing…

A few minutes later Bob came out with his towel, walked over and got in the shower. The little guy moved to the other side of the room. As I watched him, I realized that he and Bob were the same size, but the little guy seemed smaller. I think he wanted to disappear, like go back to the womb. I started reading a hard cover I'd found, about a man in a mental hospital. I also found a detective novel and I saw one about Thirty Days to a Better Vocabulary; we'll see if I have a better vocabulary in thirty days. I took them back to my cell. Then returned back to the table to resume the game, Bob had finished his shower and was shuffling the cards.

"We'll start a new hand," he said.

Tommy came over and sat down. "What da hell happen back there?"

"I was fixing a sandwich from the box my sister brought, when it started to rain. I looked around to see what in the hell was going on, that fucker was pissing all over the place. He's lucky I didn't kill him," Bob said.

"You mean he was standing there just pissing over everything?" I asked.

"No, he must have been dreaming. He was lying there happy as a lark, pissing straight up in the air. I came unglued."

"Has he got a name?" I asked.

"Hell, I don't know. If he does I never heard it," Bob said.

"It's Albert," Tommy said.

We played cards for an hour or so; then I decided to go see what was happening with the book I'd picked up, about the mental patient.

This is June, the grand jury met in May, they won't meet again till October. Bob says this place will fill up by then. It looks like I'll be here to find out.

Albert had picked up his mattress, and moved in with Harlin, in the first cell. Harlin picked up his mattress, and moved in with Bob. So there I was with one crazy guy, one about to go crazy (Harlin, if he didn't get out in a couple weeks), an old man who didn't seem too bad as long you stayed on his right side, and a Mexican my age.

&

Six weeks I've been in this place. The days are long and hot, I mostly wear my boxer shorts. If I lie on my bunk and read during the day I don't sweat as much as I would moving around. It's still a three shower day, anyway you look at it. The first morning, they gave us half a cup of syrup, with two slices of bread, the strongest coffee I ever tasted, in a large steel cup.

"What's this shit?" I said aloud.

I took the coffee and saved half for later, but I wasn't about to eat that syrup. A week later, I was saving the syrup in a paper cup and drinking it straight. I got this sugar craving that wouldn't quit. At eleven we got lunch: beans and cornbread. That was it until the next morning. Soon I became the first in line for my coffee and syrup. I started to pick up old butts, break them open, and save the old tobacco. Then roll the tobacco up in new paper. On weekends they would throw a few drunks in the bull pen, if they had cigarettes I would try to get them, or try to make friends with them, so they'd leave me a pack or two. Most of the men would never look back; once out the door, they were gone.

Harlin got out three weeks earlier, with a promise on his lips to get me a carton of cigarettes. I actually thought he would, but after three weeks, I didn't think so. I was glad when he got out he would probably have blown before Albert.

Albert's up at midnight, paces till six in the morning. Now this guy can get on your nerves; he never talks to anyone, sleeps most of the day away. I keep thinking that I'll see them take him away in a straight jacket, but he seems to hang in there.

Another Mexican came into the cell with us. He and Tommy talked in Spanish most of the time. They said they would teach me to speak in Spanish and they tell me a few words or sentences each day. I keep a notebook of words, and keep on learning.

We've got twelve regulars that are here all the time. Five of them were in the joint up at Huntsville, the State Penitentiary. They play cards most of the time. The center cell is now known as "The Office." The occupants are the elite, or so they think.

I was always at the window at eight A.M. to watch the women go into the courthouse, and at five P.M. when they got off. The rest of the time I either read or slept. The lights were on twenty-four hours a day. One morning Bob came up to me…

"Pat, the guys are talking about you being too friendly with the Mexicans. They want you to move out of the back cell. You can go into the first cell, there's an extra bunk there."

I was sitting on the edge of the table, ankles crossed, hands on the edge,

"What! They want me to move out of my cell? Bullshit, I was there before they got here; besides I like where I'm at. Fuck'em if they don't like it," I said, getting up and moving over to the bars.

"Well, consider what I said. I think you'd be wise to do it," Bob said,

My mind was spinning trying to figure which of them would instigate this. There was Cody: he had sandy brown hair, about my size, big ears, and gray eyes set close together, large nose that had been broken at one time. He wore tan pants and shirt most of the time. In his thirty-five years, half of that time spent in jail.

Jim now, was a curly headed fellow, curls close to the skull, tall and big boned, sad brown eyes, wide mouth; he seemed to always have a two-day growth of beard, even after he shaved. He was a nice enough guy who had spent two or three years in the joint. And little Bill, he walked around in jeans, no shirt, he looked somewhat like a gorilla, hairy long arms, dark short hair. He was only five-foot-five, a hundred and sixty pounds. They had moved into Bob's cell one by one, so it became the office.

Eddie was a different sort. He was the ladies man, sandy brown hair that lies over to the side of his head, blue eyes, and a slow smile. When you look at this guy, you think he has to be the most honest person you ever met. The fact is he doesn't have a serious bone in his body; in fact he doesn't even take these people serious. Eddie is a Texan, but considers himself hip, slick, and cool. We get along fine, but it looks like he is on his way back to the joint.

The thing I noticed about these guys is that one is not bad by himself; with two, they still each have a distinct personality and they talk about the joint a lot. But with three or more, the 'attitude' appears. The Prison Mentality takes over, "Mirror, mirror on the wall, who's the baddest of them all?" When you have three or four of these guys together telling each other how bad they are, God automatically moves to their side.

I think County time is hard time, in comparison to the penitentiary. County time is dead time. When you get to the prison walls you get your personality back or you can adopt one. I've been thinking a lot about Huntsville Prison lately; these fools might send me there. Bob's been telling me a lot about Huntsville; on the good side, they have a good educational system, I could finish high school, take a college course. I started getting excited about doing that. I could even come out with a trade of some sort, the possibilities were endless. On the bad side, I could end up as someone's sweetheart. Bob says, They like young boys up there. "You're kind of ugly, but one of the guys will take a cotton to you."

"Bullshit," I said, stomping back and forth.

"Well, ya gotta get tough," he said.

☙

It was about this time that I met Les. I came out into the bullpen to get my morning coffee and dose of syrup. I noticed a couple of drunks passed out against the wall, over by the shower. One had begun sitting up, rummaging in his clothes for a cigarette. As he pulled one out, I walked over and asked, "Hey buddy, ya got an extra smoke?"

"Sure." He looked around, his bleary eyes roaming over the bars, "Where the hell am I?" he asked, sliding up against the wall.

"This is the Benton County Jail, my man," I said, kneeling down beside him.

"I must of got drunk out last night, I can't remember a damn thing," he said in a high voice, shaking his head with a crooked smile.

I lit my smoke and held his hands steady so he could light his. "You look as if you could use a cup of coffee."

"Hey! That would be great," he said, pushing his hair back with his left hand.

I went over to the little window in the door, grabbed a cup of coffee, took it to my cell, came back and got two more, one for him, one for the guy next to him. When I got back, he was washing his face at the sink. The man was six foot, a hundred seventy pounds, gray eyes, slim nose, with trimmed mustache, the hair used to be blond, but was turning gray. He was in his early fifties.

I handed him his coffee. His friend was still passed out so I sipped on the friend's coffee.

"Thanks," he said, holding the cup with both hands.

We went over by the bars and sat down on the floor. His shirt was open half way up, his chest was aflame, covered with little sores, pus oozing out of them.

"What the hell happened to your chest?" I asked, pointing at the sores.

"Shrimp poisoning. I've been working on the shrimp boats and this goes along with the job; when you're heading shrimp, the juice squirts back at you. If you don't wash right away, this is the result." He motioned toward his chest with both hands.

"It looks like shit. How long you been working the shrimp boats?"

"Not long, a few months or so. I've been here a couple of weeks. The boat I'm on came down here from Brownsville. I worked a couple of other boats, but had a little trouble with the crew or the captain. This boat is pretty good; the crew gets along fine, but if I don't get out of here in a couple days I'll miss the boat. They're heading back to Brownsville."

"Where's Brownsville?" I asked.

He looked at me as if I didn't have good sense, reached down and picked a cigarette out of his pack.

"Don't mind if I do," I said.

He handed me one, struck a match and lit both smokes I sipped my coffee while he talked.

"I take it you're not from around here? Les asked.

I shook my head, "I'm from Michigan, just traveling through."

"Brownsville is at the mouth of the Rio Grande River across from old Mexico. Its beautiful country down there, you're right on the Gulf of Mexico. Working on the shrimp boats is a great life for a drunk. The jobs are fairly easy to get, there's room and board, and the pay isn't that bad. When you're out on the water most of the time ya can't get a drink. Gives a man time to get healthy. Jails are another way to keep from drinking, but you get a pale complexion. The food's not that good either and the pay stinks," he said.

"So what you're telling me is you are a drunk, huh," I said.

"Hell yes, I been pouring it down for years; to look at me now you wouldn't know I was a doctor. Fifteen years ago I had a good practice, a wife, two kids. The wife and kids left, then the business left. I started roaming, always drinking. I found my way over to Vegas. A man can live the good life in Las Vegas, if he learns how to gamble, treats it like a business. I would go gamble just like I would go to a job, including regular hours. A person can't get greedy though; you have to know when to quit. Hell, I had a two hundred dollar a month apartment, hundred dollar suits. I'd be living high on the hog, then go bust. Then be washing dishes for a dollar an hour, trying to get a stake in order to start over. The best jobs when you're trying to get a stake, is as a shill.

"A shill?" I asked.

"A shill is the guy sitting at a card table playing with the house's money, a fill-in. When things get slow they put in an extra person to fill space, that's all, but it pays good money. The last time I went bust I woke up on a freight train in El Paso, wandered on down to the Gulf and here I am." He watched me over his cup as he sipped his coffee,

"What about you, how did you come to this fate?" he asked.

So I told him about myself, the year and a half in Ohio, the trip down to New Orleans, my jaunt up into Texas, the chase with the cops. Before I knew it, I was telling him everything about myself. The guy was just easy to talk with. We must have talked for a couple of hours. It's funny how you can talk to a hundred people and never say a word that means anything, then you meet a person and everything has a meaning. That's how it was with Les. Over the next few days we became good friends. We would sit up half the night talking about the things he did, and the great adventures I would have. We talked of philosophy, religion, politics. I think we covered every phase of life. He knew a little about everything, and a whole lot about other things.

❧

One day I came out into the bullpen and a few of the guys were over at the bars talking to a new face, a trustee. As I came up I could hear them talking about Huntsville. I got my coffee and started listening to the talk. Bud was a new trustee, he was big and bulky, a two-day growth of beard, he leaned up against the bars chewing on a stogie as he continued, "I smacked his head on the bar, his nose broke. I thought it was his whole head the way it sounded. The next thing I knew there were cops all over the place; when I woke up in the morning the judge gave me ninety days. I been off parole for over a year now, I ain't going back to that joint, shit I'd go stir crazy. Besides, everybody likes me around here; see how fast I made trustee." As he spoke he shifted the cigar around with his tongue.

"Well, Bud, you can do ninety days standing on your head. Hell, the last time I saw you, you were doing six years in the penitentiary," Cody said, pushing the sandy hair back over the large ears. "It looks like you've picked up a couple of pounds in the last few years."

"Yeah, the good life," Bud said.

I started to turn and go back to my cell, when I heard Bud say, "Did ya hear 'bout the girl they're bringing in today?"

I turned back, the others looked on expectantly. When he was sure he had our attention, he gave a slow smile and said, "They had an all-points out for them. Did some robberies up north of here; anyway, the boyfriend tried to rob a bar and got hisself caught. In the meantime, she's down the street and hauls ass. By the time they figger there's a woman around, she's long gone. They put the hounds out after her, and guess what? She outrun them dogs, you believe that? They picked her up on this ol' road half wore out. Clothes all ripped up, but still had fight left in her. It took four cops to bring her in."

"No shit," Bob said." What happened to the boyfriend, they got him downstairs?"

"Yeah, he's down there, but who gives a shit' bout him; it's her that I'm waitin for…"

"What the hell you going to do with her? It's a man she wants, someone like me, you'll see," Cody said.

"Bullshit! You're behind the bars," Bud said, "I'm on the other side of them. I can see it now; she just backs that ol' ass up to the bars, and I drive it on home, YES!"

He clenched both fists together and tucked them into his chest. He started dancing there in the hallway with his invisible girl, and danced right down the hall out of sight. Then he stepped back into sight and blew us a kiss as he disappeared.

"I think I would like to be a trustee," I said, walking back to my cell.

I picked up my book and lay down, blowing smoke rings into the air, trying for the perfect ring. Man, I wanted out. Thinking about women always made me feel sad. It wasn't going to happen today so the hell with it. I started reading.

❧

I stepped into Bob's cell. Bob was sitting on the bottom bunk, Cody lay on the top bunk, Jim on the other.

"Bob, ya got anything to read? I'm running short on reading material," I said.

"No," Bob said, not looking at me.

Cody jumped off the top bunk, his face up close to mine. He had a twitch under his left eye, for a second I thought he might bite.

"I want you out of this cell right now, you snitch. If I catch you in here again I'll cut your heart out," he said.

I stood there, my stomach tightening into a ball. I knew what a snitch label would do to me. Jim sat up on his bunk…

"What the hell are you talking about? I'm no snitch," I said.

"The words out on you, boy. Now get out!" Jim said.

"What! You're not going to give me a chance to defend myself?" I said.

Jim ran a hand through his hair, and pointed with the other one, "Out!" he said.

I looked down at Bob, he shook his head in agreement with Cody and Jim. I stood there in disbelief. I turned to leave and said. "Fuck you guys."

I went back to my cell and lay down pondering what I was going to do about this predicament. I sat back up and grabbed my tobacco to roll a cigarette. Les was standing in the doorway,

"Well, you can look at it in a couple of ways. All you have is a month and half till you go to court, or you could move up to the first cell. That's what this is all about, you living back here with the Mexicans. You're not following their procedure."

"You think that's what this is about, huh?" I sat there chewing on my lower lip then lit the cigarette.

"Sure," he said, "It's like when you were a kid back in Detroit. It's a territorial thing. That's the way gangs are. You do it their way or you don't do it. These five guys constitute a gang and you're on their shit list."

I stood up and started pacing. "Well fuck 'em! I'm not moving."

"I don't have any words of wisdom for you. You'll have to walk yourself through this thing. I'll be getting out in a week or so, I can bring you some smokes, and maybe we can connect when you get out."

"Ya know, I would really like that. We could head out to California or even down to old Mexico. Hell, I hear the women are beautiful and tequila flows freely," I said.

Les and I sat there and talked for an hour or so. That was the thing about Les; I always felt good when we talked. I don't know if I kept his spirit up, but am sure he kept mine up.

Later, I walked out to the bullpen, everything seemed normal. The guys at the card game ignored me, but that didn't bother me much. I went over to the bars and watched the street below, smoked a cigarette, then went back to my cell and read.

❧

Roberto came in showing bright teeth in his chunky face. He was nineteen, short, with Levis on, no shirt. He'd been out in the bullpen playing dominoes. He was a friendly little guy and I liked him. "Que paso, hombre?"

"Nada," I said.

"Did you know Bud's out in the bullpen?"

"No shit, he's a trustee, how in hell did he get in here?" I asked, sitting up on my bunk.

"The door opened and in walked Bud, like he had the run of things," Roberto answered.

I got up off my bunk and walked out to the bullpen. Sure enough, Bud was sitting there telling jokes to some of the guys. I listened a while, then went back to my book. Roberto was putting on his shirt as I stepped into the cell.

"You coming out? he asked. Bud brought a bag of candy bars with him.

"No, I think I'll read," I said.

Roberto went out the door as I sat down to read. I could hear the laughter from the back cell. In a minute I was caught up in the story. Twenty minutes later I heard this commotion, and running feet stomping down the hallway. I sat up and jumped to the door to see what was happening. Bud had Roberto pushed up into a corner of the hall outside the cell. Roberto was still laughing.

"You little bean eater, I oughtta break both those hands of yours. Didn't your mother teach you good manners? You can't stick those grubby hands in my bag of candy."

The hallway was in semi-darkness as I stood watching. I started to turn back into the cell when Roberto let out a scream. Bud had given him a swift kick with a knee to the groin, as two candy bars dropped to the floor. Bud looked down at the candy bars, then stepped on them, grinding them with his foot. Roberto was down on his knees. Bud held onto Roberto's shirt collar as he turned his head to spit tobacco juice at my feet. His eyes caught mine and held them a second. He kicked Roberto again.

"Don't you think that's enough," I said. "You brought the candy in for everybody, didn't ya?"

He let go of Roberto's shirt and turned towards me. I saw the glint of the blade before Bud had it all the way out. I stepped back a pace, the knife poised in front of me.

"You don't want to fuck with me, northen boy. I'll be more than will'n to cut those balls off of ya."

I stood there totally surprised by the knife. Roberto sat limp at Bud's feet, crying as Bud waved the knife menacingly…

"Hey man, I don't want all this trouble; what the hell you doing in here with a knife anyways?" I said, backing away, my hands up as if pushing air.

Then you go to that bunk and set yourself down, let me talk to this Mex awhile."

Bud bent over Roberto with the blade under his earlobe, "Ya know, I could fuck ya up real good now, don't-cha, boy?"

"Yes," Roberto whimpered.

"You say Sir! when you talk to me, boy."

Bud got down on one knee, putting his mouth in close, and started whispering, knife pressed into the neck, talking real low to the crying Roberto.

Minutes passed. I hated this indecision. And then it was over. Bud just got up and went back to the bullpen. It dawned on me that the whole cell-block had been silent. Everybody had been waiting in anticipation for this drama to play out.

I went out to help Roberto to his feet. He walked bent over, hands between his legs.

"A good kick in the nuts lets you know you're still alive and well," I said.

He didn't think that was funny. I boosted him up onto the bunk and he turned to the wall, silent. I reached down behind my mattress and got a smoke. As I lit it my eyes landed on the smashed candy bars in the hallway. I stepped out, picked them up, and put them at the end of my bunk.

❧

I stood at the bars looking down at the street. Bob was sitting at the table playing solitaire. There were just the two of us. I pulled out my tobacco and sat down to roll a few cigarettes, "Bud got a little nuts tonight, didn't he?" I said.

"You brought it on yourself," Bob said.

"Whadaya mean, I brought it on myself?"

"Don't ya get it, man, that was for your benefit. You should of moved from that cell when I told ya to," Bob said.

I finished rolling a cigarette and lit it, inhaling deeply, and almost choked, "Ya mean that was about me not moving out of the cell? That was a pretty mean fucking thing to do, especially to Roberto."

"Best he learn now than in the joint. He's still a Mexican, even with you living back there."

"I can't believe this shit."

"Well, believe it. I don't think you're going up to the joint this time, but if you ever do, don't forget who you are, white boy."

There was no more to be said. I stood and went over to the bars to watch the street below. A car would pass now and then, but all was quiet.

Something changed that night; there was no more grab-assing around, the ha-ha'ing was gone. I started keeping to myself. Everything else seemed to go on as normal, the card games, the bullshitting. Les and I still talked on into the night. Then his day came to get out. He promised to bring a carton of smokes. I said I'd meet him over on the coast when I got out. Good to his word, he showed two days later, half drunk, with a carton of cigarettes. We agreed to meet up when I got out.

℣

The big day arrived. They said to be ready by seven. We marched out in single file, to another holding tank. I didn't get my morning coffee, and only had one smoke. We sat there all morning waiting. No court. Lunch time came and went. No food. By six o'clock that evening I was starving. Eating only one meal a day, I kind of got used to it. I thought they might come and take me back to the cell and do it again tomorrow, but around seven-thirty I heard keys in the door. They took me into the courtroom and had me sit at a side table.

The judge was an old guy, small, with gray hair. A pair of half glasses sat on the bridge of his nose. He was hearing Tommy's case. He looked over the top of his glasses at Tommy and gave him two years probation. His family got up and started hugging him. The judge decided to take a break. Tommy looked over at me with a big smile. I gave him a thumb's up sign, but my guts were churning, waiting for this judge to get off the stick.

The judge walked back into the court room a few minutes later and took his seat, shuffled a few papers around, then called my name. I walked out and stood in front of him.

He looked down at me, leaning over his bench and said, "What do you think, have you done enough time on this thing?"

"Yes sir," I said, looking about five inches below the top of his bench.

"Why is it you northen boys come down here without a job or money. You have no choice but to get into trouble. I am going to give you a year's probation. What I want is for you to make restitution on this check and head yourself back up north where your folks are. Don't let me see you again or you'll do that year."

"Yes sir. I'll take care of it," I said, feeling shaky all over.

The next thing I knew I was standing on the steps of the courthouse, dumbfounded, not knowing what to do. For a minute there I wanted to pound on the door so I could eat and sleep in my own bed, but it only lasted half a minute. I knew the street in front of the courthouse ran over to the city of Freeport on the Gulf of Mexico so I ran across the street and put my thumb out. Freedom smelled great again, even on an empty stomach.

CHAPTER FOUR

The Fishing Port

It was a warm October night as I stood looking out over the bay. I was standing on the docks of a small fishing port on the Gulf of Mexico. I was elated, feeling great. It had just hit me that I was really out of jail. Two great blue herons were standing in the water just off shore, fifty feet apart. One stood straight up, neck erect, head high, the other was in position to strike, head low, as if frozen in time. I watched, fascinated.

Minutes passed. One of the herons stood poised, then struck. Triumphant, his head came up and back as he swallowed a small fish.

I looked out over the calm waters of the bay. The offshore winds had died down for the day. The fishing boats lay at their moorings, rocking gently. Five or six docks were laid out with fingers running off them. The lights all around held my attention. Most of the fishermen had gone wherever fishermen go at night. I was hoping to run into someone I knew from the jail, or maybe even Les, though I wasn't counting on that. I thought he would be back in Brownsville by now.

I started down the ramp to the docks. The tide seemed to be half way out. A man was walking toward me. He had a long beard and graying hair, with a sea bag slung over his shoulder.

"How's it going?" I asked, stopping to talk.

"All right," he said, and kept walking.

"Do you know anyone looking for a hand?" I asked, turning around as he passed me. "I'm looking for a job."

"You might try the *Linda Lu*. I heard yesterday she needed a hand," he pointed over to the south waving his arm, "She's on Dock Three."

"Hey thanks," I said, "I'll check it out."

I watched him walking up the ramp, wondering where the hell dock three was. I finished walking the dock I was on, and then went back up to look at the number. Seven. I started walking in an easterly direction until I came to dock three. Most of the boats had lights on inside to keep out the dampness. I strolled along looking for signs of life – not too many people this time of night. Then I spotted the Linda Lu all lit up. I walked slowly by, trying to spot somebody aboard – nobody – then a head popped up and moved towards the back of the cabin. Aha! There is somebody there. I stepped over to the boat and knocked on her steel hull. She was about sixty feet long, with a twenty-foot cabin. The nets were sprawled on the back deck. I called out, "Is anybody aboard?"

The same head I'd seen earlier stuck itself out the doorway and peered down at me. I recognized that face right off. The first time I'd seen it, he was passed out against a cell wall of the Benton County Jail.

"Who's there?" he yelled

I stepped out into the light so he could see me. "How you been, Jim? I haven't seen you in couple of months," I said.

"Is that you, Pat? When the hell did you get out? Come on aboard. Hell, it's good to see ya. Never thought I'd see ya on the outside, though," he said in that southern draw of his.

I grabbed the rail and put one foot on the deck, pulled myself up and over, saying, "I just got out an hour ago. Heard there might be a job on the Linda Lu. So here I am."

"Sorry about that Pat, we hired a guy yesterday. But you're in good hands on this boat. Gawd, what were you in there for, six months or so?" he asked, tossing his head back, getting the sandy hair out of his face.

Jim was six foot tall with a ruddy complexion. Too much open air, too much booze, made him appear as if he had just had a drink, and maybe he had. Jim always looked like that in jail, where he never had a drink.

"Yeah, too damn long, I said. It amazes me how much I have to force myself to move forward; I'm so used to fifty feet and then a wall. How you been anyway?"

"Good. You want a beer, or something to eat? I got it all. We just loaded up on food this afternoon. We're heading out on a ten day trip tomorrow, I guess."

"Man, I haven't had any food all day. I was wondering what I was going to do."

"Well, ol' son, you're in the right place. Come on in and let Jimbo show you how it's done."

He seemed genuinely glad to see me. I know I was glad he appeared out of nowhere.

☙

I was sitting there, stuffed for the first time in six months as best I could remember. We were on our third beer, Jim was telling me about his fishing days in Mississippi. We heard a loud yell from out on deck and looked up at the same time. A bald head appeared in the doorway, his body off to one side. The face had a big mustache and an earring in one ear, bright eyes, and a big smile.

"What are you two doing sitting there? The party is about to begin, let's go," he said.

"I've got to get this engine done tonight," Jim said.

"Bullshit! You guys aren't leaving till late tomorrow afternoon, so get your shit together and let's party. The man stepped into the cabin, all six-foot-four of him.

"Well, what the hell, ya talked me into it. You'll have to back me up when Cap'n Jack finds out I didn't finish the engine," Jim said.

"No sweat. Who's your friend here?"

"Oh, this is Pat. I met him in jail a month or so ago, he just got out a couple of hours ago. He's been in for six months," Jim said. "By the way, this big asshole is Dave, they call him Crazy Dave. Come on, Pat, let's go chase down some women."

Jim got up and went down below deck to change his shirt and get something, probably his wallet. I sat there unsure as to what to do. I was flat broke. I waited. Dave went over and got a beer out of the box. Jim reappeared and said, "Let's go." I stood up and put my palms up and shook my head, "I'm flat."

"Don't sweat the small stuff, come on," Jim said, grabbing the rail and looking at Dave.

Dave downed the beer in one gulp, "Ahhhhh, I'm ready now." The three of us jumped off the boat and headed up the dock, looking for some action.

☙

I was glad I'd had some food. If I hadn't eaten, those three beers would probably have knocked me on my ear. As it was, I was feeling pretty good. A tavern sat on the corner across the street from the docks. An earthy smell of rain was in the air as we crossed the street. We stepped into the bar and ordered a round of beers. A pretty blonde brought the beer over to the table we were sitting around. Her name was Peggy. The jukebox was wailing out an old Hank Williams song; he was in love with a pretty woman and she didn't love him back. So was I, after seeing the blonde. (In love with a pretty woman, that is.) Ten or twelve fishermen were sitting at the bar. A couple of women and one man sat at a table

We were seated near the door. Dave put his arm around Peggy's waist and started telling his sad story right off.

"Peggy, I have this problem, and it's a sad, sad thing,"

"What's that, honey?" asked the blonde.

"It's that bed of mine. It's so big I can't keep it warm. I need a soft-skinned woman like yourself to be in it, How 'bout after work tonight?"

"Sweetie, you're the biggest thing around, and I love that bald head. If it weren't for that no account husband of mine, I'd be in that bed of yours in no time. You'll have to tell him that the next time you see him, course he won't believe a word of it. He's due back in a couple of hours."

"You be sure to tell him I was asking after him. How the kids doing, anyway?"

"Chrissie and Morgan are over at my mother's. How long you boys in for?"

"Just long enough to get ice and supplies – probably leave tomorrow evening. This here fellow is Pat, a friend of ours looking for a boat. Hear of any deck hands that have ended up jail, or just went amuck?"

"No, not lately," she said. "Did hear something about the Katie Ann, but she left this evening, I think."

"Well, if you hear anything, keep us in mind. In the meantime, we're going to live it up a little. Where in hell is all them women at, anyway? All you have here is dried up fishermen. I'm ready to howl, like an ol' coyote dog."

Peggy stood there with her hand on Dave's shoulder, looked over at Jim and said, "You take this big ol' horny toad down to the Easy Pickins. I don't want any more of his foolishness around here. I'm sure you'll all get laid down there," she said. "You can leave Pat here, he's kind of shy and quiet. I like that."

I had a beer bottle upended, taking a drink. I glanced over at her and set the bottle down.

"Pay attention now, I'm not a good friend of your husband's and I been in jail for six months."

She threw her hands up, and shook her head. "Men, they're all the same, not a good one amongst em," and walked back to the bar, giving me a quick smile over her shoulder.

A couple of the men at the bar turned around and one said, "How was that last trip you guys made. Do any good?"

"Yeah, 'bout thirty boxes," Dave said. "And you?"

"I'd like to say the same, but all we got was fourteen and a little change," he said.

"You better rub that lucky piece or take a couple links out of that tickler chain; you're dragging too deep," Dave said and gave up a big smile. "You all come out with me an' I'll show ya the ropes."

"Ah bullshit," he said, as he turned back to the bar.

Dave had been sitting on the back two legs of his chair. He came forward with a bang, and yelled for another round. He started talking with Jim about shrimp and nets, boats, sharks, holes in nets, sewing nets, and rigging. It hit me that I didn't have a clue what they were talking about. I had never seen a shrimp boat till a couple of hours ago, let alone worked on one. I just kept quiet and listened, while drinking the beer. My mind kind of wandered off a minute, focused on the music coming out of the jukebox, and then I heard the word "jail." My mind snapped back, Dave was asking me what I'd been in jail for.

"Do you really want to hear my story?" I asked, tipping up my bottle.

"Sure, there's nothing like a good story."

I told them about hitchhiking down to New Orleans, then up the Gulf Coast to Texas – about Jewel and Harlin, the shooting, the jail. When I had finished they were laughing at parts I didn't think were funny, but when I saw it through their eyes, it was pretty funny at that. I would have to quit taking my shit so seriously.

"Drink up and let's head down to the Easy Pickins and see what's hap-nin'," Dave said.

We upended our beers then got up to go. Dave left a good size tip. Jim stopped me at the door and handed me a twenty-dollar bill.

"Pay me when you get on your feet."

"Hey man, sure do appreciate this. I'll get it back to you as soon as I can," I said.

✑

The rain was coming down lightly as we stepped out onto the street; it had been raining about an hour or so. As we walked out of the light I could see the gathering clouds, moving in quickly. A storm was on its way. I turned my face up to the dark sky and let rain wash the drunkenness from me. I felt light-headed, money in my pocket, my stomach full, and half drunk. I felt wonderful. I took a step and jumped two feet up in the air and yelled, "I'm going to get laid tonight!"

"I like the way you think, boy," Dave said, coming up behind me.

The street was getting muddy; potholes were all over the place. The three of us went down the muddy road jumping puddles in the rain; it was a great night.

We came up to the Easy Pickins on the west side of the building, a little sign over the door blinked, "open." Dave went in, Jim and I followed. I found myself at the end of the bar; it ran the width of the room. I saw an exit at the other end of the bar. There is a smell that old bars have, of beer spilled days ago, human sweat, tears too; just people living, loving and drinking. My nostrils took offense at first, then old memories took over. I loved that smell. The joint was jumping, people talking loudly. Men and women sat at the bar, mostly men, some standing. Tables were situated on each side of the room and a packed dance floor was in the center. Jerry Lee Lewis was screaming out 'Great Balls of Fire'. Most of the men looked like fishermen, a few cowboys, everyone seemed to be having fun. I noticed another exit at the front of the room.

Dave pushed his way over to the bar and ordered a double round of beers. Jim grabbed an empty table and sat down. I sat on the other side bouncing to the music, yelling "This is dee place man."

A little blonde haired girl was under Dave's arm as he made his way over to the table, three bottles of beer in each hand, "Take this here young'un, Pat, and get to dancin."

Now, normally I am a wallflower, but after a six-pack I become a hell of a dancer. I looked at the girl, my eyes all aglow, "How about it, girl, should we get it working?"

"Let's do it," she said, turning toward the dance floor.

The floor was ours for the next few minutes. All I could see were those blue eyes and rosy cheeks. Carl Perkins was singing "Blue suede shoes." When the song finished I followed her back to the table, grabbed a beer and drank half of it down, and took a deep breath, put my arm around her waist, and asked.

"What's your name, little girl?"

She took the bottle from her lips and said, "I'm Cindy. I think we should get back out on the floor and keep on danc'n'."

Dave was talking to a black-haired beauty at the next table, and Jim was walking through the crowd with a beer in hand, looking over the possibilities. So, back out on the dance floor Cindy and I went. A half hour later I fell into a chair and yelled, "Enough, I have to catch up on the beer drinking!"

Cindy gave me a big smile and ran a hand through my wet hair, "You rest, baby, I have ta go to the little girl's room."

I watched her slip through the people as I caught my breath, picked up a bottle, downed most of it. Jim came over, "You seem to be doing all right, man."

"Yeah man, I'm in love all right."

"That's lust my boy, healthy lust."

Jim told me he danced a few times, but nothing exciting was going on. I was feeling good, my face felt flushed, so I drank down a few more beers. Cindy came back and sat beside me. Dave had disappeared. Jim was talking about the money he would make on this next trip. That's when I heard the yelp from across the room. I jumped up to get a better look, then started moving toward the commotion. I was in the center of the dance floor on the edge of the crowd that had gathered, when the group of onlookers suddenly opened up and this guy came sailing out head first, a couple feet off the floor. Through the split in the crowd I could see Dave holding a dark-haired fellow up off the ground a foot or two. Dave was laughing and seemed to be having a good time. There was a guy between us who was about to hit Dave over the back of the head with a chair. I quickly stepped up and grabbed the chair. "Hold on there podner," I said, as I jerked on the chair. Then, the left side of my head exploded. I'd seen the blur a split second before. I shook my head and looked to see who hit me. Jim was on top of a guy punching with all he had. I turned back to my immediate problem. I had let go of the chair for a minute and in that time my blond-haired assailant had lifted the chair over his head and it was coming down toward me. I leaned over to my right and took it off the shoulder as I made a lunge for his waist. He toppled over. I came up punching as fast and hard as I could. Someone jumped on my back. I felt as if I was wading through mud. I tried to look up. The whole place seemed to be in an uproar. For the next few minutes I kept punching, people kept holding me down. I was trying to get into the clear. At one point I thought I heard a shot, but wasn't sure. It felt like two people were on my back and someone else holding my legs. As I struggled to get loose, somebody yelled, "COPS!" And then I was free. I stumbled to my feet looking around. Jim was a few feet away, nose bloody, hair hanging down over his eyes. "You better haul ass, the cops'll be here in a minute. You don't wanta end up back in jail. I'll catch up with ya later." Jim headed for the side door.

I ran for the door on the other side, the room was almost empty. I shot through the door and into a rail on the porch and over I went, my breath knocked out of me. I lay on my back, the rain hitting me full in the face. I lay there a moment wondering what the hell had happened, the rain felt good. I didn't want to move, then I remembered the law was after me. I got up and stumbled down the alley as fast as I could go. I was weaving down one side, then the other. The next thing I know I'm drowning in all this water, I kept flopping around then getting up and falling again. I seemed to be in some kind of hole, and couldn't get out. I kept trying, but I was exhausted; I felt somebody pulling on me, then I'm lying on my side, "Fuck it! I'm too tired to give a shit." I passed out.

☙

I opened one eye and looked around. "Ah, shit!" I was sitting in a six-by-eight cell, my mind going in ten different directions. I heard someone in another room say, "He's awake now." I was thinking of what that judge said to me, just hours ago, about that year in jail. My heart was racing, I got up as close to the bars as I could get, listening for any conversation from the other room. I heard some movement, but not much else. Finally I heard someone say, "Should I run a make on him?" Then a deeper voice said, "Naw, if we ran a make on every fishermen we picked up there wouldn't be any more fishermen. Just give him some coffee and cut him loose. Tell him next time it's his ass."

I didn't listen for any more, that's what I wanted to hear. I had a big smile on my face thinking that as soon as I got out I would make a beeline out of town. My clothes were still wet, I would need a change. I hoped Jim had an extra pair of jeans. Fifteen minutes later I was on the street, heading down towards the docks.

Jim and Dave were walking up the dock when I started down. Jim looked up and saw me and started laughing. Dave grabbed me in a big bear hug and said, "We thought you were a goner. I didn't think you would see the light of day for a year or more."

"Well, I lucked out. They were pretty decent, didn't even check up on me. The chief said if they checked every fisherman out there would be no more fishermen. That tells you something about shrimpers," I said, "They're all outlaws!"

"I'm glad to see everything came out all right. Dave and I are going up for breakfast; come on along and get something to eat," Jim said.

"Say, man, you got anything I could wear while I wash these clothes? I asked.

"Sure, I'll be right back." He headed off down the dock.

Dave still had an arm around me. He pulled me up close and said, "You did pretty good last night Pat, you're tougher than you look." He shook me around like I was a big teddy bear.

I broke loose from his grip, "You bastard, you almost got me killed last night." I said, laughing. "How in hell did that fight get started anyway? Everything was going along fine. I was just about to get laid and then the shit hit the fan."

"Those two jumped me because I was messing with their women. Some people can't take a joke. Besides most shrimpers just live to fight. If you don't like to fight, you had best stay ashore, my friend," Dave said.

"Hell, I don't mind fighting, but I'm more of a lover than a fighter, especially if I'm about to get laid," I said, punching him in the shoulder, then dancing back like a boxer with my guard up. We were standing there laughing when Jim came up carrying a pair of pants. "Here ya go, hoss, the washers are up there in that little white building," he said, pointing up behind me.

I looked up to where he was pointing and saw the little building, off to the right. I also saw a café and asked, "Is that where you'll be eating breakfast?"

"That's the place," he said.

"OK. I'll meet you there in a few," I said and took off up the dock.

I put the clothes in the washer and set the timer, then stepped out onto the dock and headed east along the fish buildings. Two big buildings with large bay doors on the front, with two workers unloading a shrimp boat. There was a small crane on the side of the dock with a cable, lifting a steel box out of the fish hold. The box was loaded with shrimp. I watch them for a minute then moved on down the dock to the café. A forklift carrying a box passed me as I opened the door and walked into the café.

The restaurant was full of fishermen having breakfast. A counter to my left had six stools, all full, and eight tables, one was empty. Jim and Dave were in the back. Jim stood up when he saw me, acted like he was pouring coffee into an invisible cup and pointed toward the wall at the end of the counter. I walked over and got myself a cup of coffee, then made my way over to the table. Lights with copper shades hung from the ceiling. The wall behind the grill was faced with copper, giving everything a golden glow. Jim nodded his head as I sat down. He continued shoveling eggs and grits into his mouth, thoroughly enjoying himself. Dave raised his fork and kept on eating. An older waitress with short blonde hair and earrings that hung two inches below her ears took my order of ham and eggs. I sipped hot coffee and lit a cigarette, thinking how grateful I was not to be in jail.

Jim finished his breakfast and said, "I haven't heard of anybody who needs a hand yet, but I know if you hang around a couple days you'll pick up on something."

I flicked the ashes off my cigarette. Spinning the ashtray around in circles, I said, "I don't think so, that was too close last night. I've got to put some distance between me and that jail. I'm heading down to Brownsville as soon as I eat. With any luck I should be able to find a boat and I'll be five hundred miles from that jail." I put the smoke out as my food arrived.

"Well shit, I wish I was going with you, but I'll be down that way myself in a month or two. Tell you what, I'll give you the names of a couple of friends of mine. You never know, they might need a header. The insurance laws just changed; you almost need a third man if you're going to have insurance," Jim said. "What you do when you get there is head over to Port Isabel, find the Perfect Fisheries. They have about ten boats. Ask for Captain Rocky on the *Perfect Dawn,* or go to the *Perfect Girl* and talk to Captain Dan. Tell them ol' Jimbo sent you round." He took out a paper and started writing it down for me. "Here, you find these guys and get on with them and you'll be in like Flynn," Jim said, handing me the paper.

We had a little more coffee and talked small talk. I made up my mind it was now or never, so we said our goodbyes; after which I got up and went after my clothes.

On the highway I stood with thumb out. There was no action, so I took out the paper Jim had given me. "Rocky, huh. Well, Port Isabel here I come," I said aloud to no one in particular.

CHAPTER FIVE

Boys Town

R ocky was tall, lean, big-boned, and had a large nose that probably had been broken at one time or another. He wore a large mustache, trimmed at the edge of the mouth. The brown eyes looked through you. He always wore a baseball cap on the back of his head, brown hair hanging out – the "nice guy" look. Otherwise the cap was down over his eyes – the "serious" look. Rocky's story was that he was from upstate New York. He had a wife and kid up there that he left after getting into trouble with the law. He then wandered south until he got to the Texas coast.

I had made it to the Texas border, at the mouth of the Rio Grande. Brownsville on the United States side, Matamoras on the Mexican side. Both towns had a population of about twenty thousand people. Fifteen miles northeast of Brownsville was Port Isabel, a smaller town of three thousand. Port Isabel still had dirt roads running through it – a fishing port. It had four or five bars, one local store, and a couple of cafes. Most people worked the fishing industry. Port Isabel had three or four cops, a quiet Mexican town in the U.S. Shrimp companies were lined up all along the harbor. They had big bay doors through which you walked to get to the docks. Boats were tied three and four abreast. Located along the docks were Pedro's Fisheries, Perfect, and Ortega's. The docks were eight feet wide, on pilings. People were busy all around…nets hung from the masts, men were cleaning and sewing on nets, forklifts moving fish boxes here and there. Everything looked exciting!

I landed a job on a Perfect boat. Perfect Fisheries had twelve boats. This one was sixty-five feet long, wooden hulled, named *Perfect Girl.* She needed paint, but otherwise seaworthy. We had just finished an eight-day trip. After cleaning up and getting into some clothes that didn't smell like fish, I headed for the border. I caught up with two guys in an old green Chevy. They had been working another Perfect boat. I jumped in the back seat.

"Que pasa, hombres?" I asked.

"Well, ol' Jeff here is going to Brownsville to catch a bus. Me, I'm heading for Boys Town," Mick said, turning to look at me.

"That's where I'm heading too," I said, "It's time to get fucked up!"

Mick, the driver, was blond and bulky, with a quick smile, a cigarette dangling from his left fingers, wrist gently on the steering wheel. He paused as if to say something, then dropped the gear in first and we were off. Jeff turned and looked at me.

"What the fuck happened to you?" I asked, surprised.

Jeff was a tall, lanky fellow with prominent cheekbones, which were now under a black eye and swollen lip. The dark hair hung straight down.

"That Cap'n Rocky busted me one, then kicked me off the boat. Something I said at the bar last night, I guess. It was pretty drunk out. Anyway, he's one mean son-of-a-bitch. If you ever run into him, stay out of his way! He lives to fight. So, I'm off to California. I hear they have women trees out there. When you want one you just pluck her from a tree."

"So you're really taking off, huh?" I asked, leaning back into the seat.

"Ah sure as hell am. If'n you want a job, the '*Perfect Dawn*' needs a hand. I'm sick of this fishin." He looked thoughtful a minute, then turned toward the front of the car.

As we drove, I could see the palm trees strung out along the road. Mexican kids playing around the run-down shacks they lived in. Then it hit me! "If you get to L.A., go out to Venice, at the beach. I read an article in a magazine when I was down in the Benton County jail; it said the Beats hang out there. All night coffee houses. That's where it's happening. When I head out, that's my next stop, free love…jazz…poetry, parties all night, dope, that's for me." I said, putting my hands behind my head, stretching out my back, watching the world go by.

"Hey! that sounds good to me, I'll have to give it a try. My sister is out in L.A. someplace…Santa Monica, I think."

We were coming to the outskirts of Brownsville.

જ

As far as I know, Texas is just one big fuckin desert except for the Rio Grande valley. Heading south, out of El Paso, for a thousand miles everything is brown desert, then all of the sudden it turns green and you're in the lush fields of the Rio Grande Valley. It's about sixty miles down to Brownsville, with small towns dotted here and there. Harlingen is the main center in the Valley, also the biggest city.

I totally fell in love with this area of Texas, with its strong north winds in winter; sometimes it would blow seventy or eighty miles an hour for three or four days. They called them "northerners." Offshore winds keep it cool in summer along the coast. An occasional hurricane blows in now and then… but this place seemed like paradise.

Brownsville is a low, sprawling town. Most buildings aren't over two stories. Eighty percent of the people are Mexican. Most of the men wear big brim straw hats – sort of a "Mexican-Western" look, and the traditional Levis and boots. The women wear long colorful skirts and blouses – shawl on the shoulder or over the head, a good percentage of them Americanized. Mexicans walk north across the bridge to work or shop. Tourists swarm all over the place, preparing to venture down into Mexico.

Mick found the bus station about three blocks from the river, pulled over to the nearest bar and we went in for a beer. Four beers later, Mick and I left, telling Jeff we'd meet him in L.A. in six months.

Mick drove across the bridge to old Mexico…check station at each end of the bridge…they just waved us through. Mexicans all over the place, lots of activity on the other side; men running around to cars, with blankets, chaleckos, sandals made from tire soles…kids with gum boxes, shoeshine boys. At one point I saw a stack of hats, five feet high, walk by with about a four-foot Mexican underneath. Everything seemed to be for sale – everyone talking a mile a minute.

We drove slowly through this menagerie. Mick made a left to try to skirt the main part of town. All the shops were open at the front; none had walls. Stuff seemed to bulge out the front onto the sidewalks. Taco stands stood every fifty feet. I spotted a place with leather goods.

"Hey Mick, pull over, I need a coat," I said. "Why don't you grab a beer and taco while I'm gone."

I left Mick in a small cantina while I went looking for a coat. I came back with a leather jacket with tassels that hung below the waist and a big tan turtleneck sweater. I checked my reflection in the window: long brown hair, curls lay on the shoulders, mustached goatee. Man, I was ready for

Boys Town. Mick and I drank three more beers and headed out.

We drove this old road south out of Matamoras, a huge dust trail behind us. It was flat country with clumps of sagebrush all around. I could see off in the distance, Boys' Town. We swung around the next curve and it was a straight shot down the center of town. From a mile back, it looked like a bunch of shacks sitting in the middle of the desert. The town was about four blocks long…neon flashing everywhere. Mick pulled up on the north side of the road, in front of the old El Paso bar. Excitement was building in my gut. We went in and ordered beers.

The El Paso was a small bar, all lit up, where girls came to take a break from the bars they worked in. Mick was telling me there are no women in town without a license – a prostitute's license. Women come from all over Mexico. Their parents sell some of the young girls. Most need money, go into debt, and the proprietor gives them two rooms…one to live in and one to work in. Not all bars furnish two rooms. They see a doctor once a week. Several hundred women worked this town. There is always debt. These women live in the fast lane. They make a lot of money and spend a lot. Quite often a gringo will come along and fall in love with one of the girls and pay off her debt. He'll take her back to the United States, marry her, then in a year or so, you see her back in the bars again. Who knows what happened?

Four or five women were in the El Paso now as we drank our beers. We joked around with them a while. I told them that I was a great "parota" (pimp) and that they would never need another. They said I could come and visit, but if I were lying they would shoot my balls off. We all laughed, but I wondered. I had an eye for one of them and made a mental note to visit her later.

Mick and I stepped out onto the boardwalk, beers in hand. What a great night. I felt as though I was amongst them – those great adventurers that I had read about. Mick leaned close and said, "I'll be back in awhile. Got to get some pot before it gets too late." The night seemed to soak him up. I stood watching the people, who was coming, who was going. I looked west to the San Luis Club on the corner, then a couple of bars, a cantina, a few taco stands. The El Gatos and Rata Muerta were across the street. The American Club (they advertised floor shows, the tourists loved them). I stayed away from the tourist spots.

I was thinking about the shrimpers I'd met; so much like the pirates of the seventeenth century. Most were wanted by the law someplace or other.

You didn't delve too deeply into their pasts.

As I stood there, a policeman walked by, "Buenos dias," I said

"Buenos noches," he smiled.

"You work too hard, my friend. Let me you buy a beer?"

"No. I have to make my rounds," he replied.

I pulled out a dollar and gave it to him. "This is for later, then!" He smiled again; the dollar disappeared as he strolled down the walk. We both knew this was bullshit, but it was good insurance. You never knew what might happen – the night was still young. If I got in a spot, hopefully the other guy would go to jail and not me. I went back inside, downed two more beers, and got ready to go, when Mick showed. "I was just going over to the San Luis to see what's happening. Did you get the weed?" I asked.

"Yeah, I got eight sticks. You know who I just seen?"

"Who?" I asked.

"Grady! He's the rig man on the *Sue Ann.* I don't know if you know him. Anyway he came over two days ago. He drove his caddy over, had two thousand dollars in his pocket. Now he can't find the car, has no money, and was walking around in his shorts! I gave him twenty bucks for a cab to get back to the boat." We walked west down the boardwalk to the corner to the San Luis bar still laughing over Grady. We could almost see ourselves in that situation.

Three Texans in their mid-twenties stood outside talking. You could tell they were getting drunk and would be obnoxious before long. They were trouble looking for a place to happen. I started into the bar.

"Hey," one of them said.

I looked back at the one doing the talking.

"You boys know where the action is?"

They saw where I was going, so I thought a minute, fuck 'em, and sent them down the street to the Rata Muerta.

Mick and I stepped into a long walkway with several arches opening into the main room. The floor was about seventy-five feet long by fifty feet wide. Half the north end had tables. A fifteen-foot alcove on the east side that fit a couple of tables, the rest was open for dancing. At the far north end was a bar that ran the full width. The first time I saw this place I thought: it could be a nightclub in New York. Fats Domino was singing "Ain't That a Shame" on the jukebox up by the bar. Rock and roll was getting big in Mexico. I stood in an archway, letting my eyes adjust to the darkness, colored light all around. I'm partial to dark bars. Five shrimpers were sitting over in the alcove, all the tables were empty. We made our way over to them.

"Que pa-soooo, hombres?" Mick said, as we walked up. "Hey Pat, you know everyone?" I shook my head. "I know Billy Dee there."

"This here is Pat," Mick said, putting his hand on my shoulder. "He works on the *Perfect Girl*. That ugly fucker over there with the blond hair is Wedo. Wedo in Spanish means blonde. You know Billy Dee, that's Rocky off the *Perfect Dawn*, and this is Cap'n Norm, my captain, who I know has some money for me. Right, Cap'n?"

"Yeah, I brought you some, but you can pick up the rest at the office tomorrow." He turned back to Rocky, "I have to get back and take a few links out of the tickler chain. I want to get out by four tomorrow afternoon. Mick, we'll ice up about noon," he said in the same breath.

"Well, you got time for one more?" Rocky looked at him, "Wedo, you hear that? Get us another round."

Wedo had been sitting talking with a girl on his lap, he jumped up. The girl caught herself on the chair before hitting the floor.

"You hear that!" he motioned with his hand to the girl. Get us a round. What are you two having?" He looked at Mick, then at me.

"Rum and coke," Mick said.

"I'll take the same," I said, pulling up a chair.

Mick grabbed a chair from another table and sat down. A girl was sitting next to Billy Dee with her arm around his shoulder. I thought what a weird picture this would make.

Billy Dee was about my height, black hair, dark eyes, mustache and shy smile. You knew women would like him. Billy Dee sat sipping his drink, ignoring the affections of the girl. Norm still had his rubber boots on. Rocky and Wedo, obviously fishermen, hadn't changed their clothes either. All the girls had evening dresses on. Wedo's girl brought the drinks back. She wore yellow taffeta, bare at the shoulders, overlayed with chiffon. She wasn't more than sixteen, pretty, with short hair. Wedo stood there, blond hair to the shoulders, mustache hung below the upper lip, his tall, lean frame doing a nervous little dance. You could see the fear in him. Rocky was using it to his advantage. The girl behind Rocky had long, dark hair. She was older and looked tired and bored. Her arm lay across the back of his chair, holding her chin up. She wore black satin.

We were laughing, drinking, talking about how much shrimp we had caught, the sharks eating holes in our nets. A few more girls came over. The third or fourth joint was being passed around. I looked over at Rocky and realized at some point that he had gone and changed clothes. I was mind tripping. The pot was distorting time.

"I would like to get into a good fight," Rocky said, hitting his left hand with his right fist.

I was laughing, feeling good. It sort of jumped out of my mouth: "I'd like a good fight too."

"Well, you're the one I'd like to fight," Rocky said, eyeing me, with a slight grin.

At that point my head cleared a little. I knew I was about to get my ass kicked. I didn't want to make an enemy of this guy. He looked menacing. It was too late to turn back. "All right…" I said, hesitating a second, "The loser buys the next round."

Rocky stood up, "We'll go out on the patio."

I took a last drink and got up from the table, grabbing onto a chair for support, followed Rocky past the east end of the bar and out the doorway onto the patio. Rocky stood there, feet firmly planted, hat pulled over his eyes, rubbing a fist into the palm of his hand. I started taking off my jacket as I walked to the side… my brain exploded…my temple throbbed. I had taken my eyes off him. I felt my wind leave as I took the next one in the gut. Then there seemed to be a problem with my nose. I saw the blood as I was going down. This huge weight was on me.

"I could fuck you up real good now," I heard him say. I lay there a second. "You hear me?" he repeated.

"Yeah," I said.

"All right then," he said, and was gone.

I sat up…blood all over the turtleneck. Somebody handed me a wet bar towel. I wiped the blood off my face and the sweater, and held it to my nose until it quit bleeding. I staggered into the room and sat at the bar, waiting for my nose to quit bleeding. I looked over at the scene where I'd been sitting. They were watching me, so I ordered everyone a round. I sat there, head down, arm outstretched on the bar. Elvis was singing in the background – "Down at the end of Lonely Street." I felt a tug on my arm. "Vienta conmigo," a woman's voice said. We went down this long hall. She opened a door and gently pushed me in. I saw the bed and fell into it, passing out.

❧

Didn't Look Back

I woke looking at a pale yellow ceiling. I sat up with a throbbing in the back of my head – lips dry, tongue thick. It felt like a rat had crawled into my mouth and died. Damn, my clothes are gone...then I saw them lying over a chair. I jumped to the chair and checked my wallet. The money was still there. I started feeling better. I looked around. The walls were green. Lace cloth hung from the ceiling to hide the walls. A small vanity with a large mirror and pictures sticking out along the side sat up against the wall. I looked at myself in the mirror. Not too bad, I thought; a half moon cut at the bridge of the nose. Thank God for hard heads. I started putting my clothes on. Boxes of jewelry (cheap stuff I'd guess) were on the vanity, women's cosmetics – the usual stuff. I was trying to find a familiar face amongst the pictures.

I walked out, down the hall to the bar. Nobody. Three men were cleaning. I headed for the street. Out on the boardwalk the light hurt my eyes. I felt something rubbing along my leg. Looking down I saw a dog – an old dog that hadn't seen a meal for a while. I looked down the street. A few old cars were parked along the boardwalk, potholes all over, big enough to swim in. Chickens seemed to have their own run. People walking up and down, laughing and joking...it all seemed normal. I walked down towards the El Paso. A newer car was parked along the walk. Two guys were passed out in the front seat and one in the back – the three Texans. One of the guys in the front had puked all over his lap. I grimaced. They'll have fun when they wake up.

I stepped into the El Paso. Billy Dee was standing at the bar.

"Que Paso, my man," I said, walking up to the bar.

"Well, you don't look too bad for wear," he said, looking me over like he couldn't believe his eyes.

"No, but a beer will straighten me right out." I ordered us a round and leaned onto the bar.

"So...what's the plan?" I asked, "You have a few days off or what?"

"Well, I don't have to go out for two or three days," he said.

"Me, I'm supposed to go this evening sometime. I'll have to give it some thought. I'm not sure I'm ready to go back yet," I said.

"Did you know Rocky went to jail last night?" he asked.

"No shit," I said,

"They only held him for a while...then let him go. He was wondering if you called them."

"What! I passed out in one of the rooms. That's the last I remember."

70

I thought a minute. "Well, some things don't come easy," I said. "Where's Rocky now?" I asked, taking a long pull on the bottle of beer I was holding.

"He went back to the boat. You should have stayed away from his ass," he said.

"Shit man…it ain't like I forced the issue. Fuck it, live and learn."

Billy ordered another round. We stood at the bar, one foot on the rail, drinking beer. Billy was talking about last night. I was thinking about how I was going to get out of this situation with Rocky. I felt this punch on my shoulder… "Why no wait for me?"

I turned around. Mexican music played in the background. A girl stood there, hands on hips, white blouse and colored print skirt, thick, long, black hair pulled back over her shoulders. She had beautiful big eyes, the lips tight, demanding an answer. I assumed she was the owner of the bed I had slept in.

"I didn't know where you were, so I came looking for you. I wanted to buy you breakfast and thank you for last night," I lied.

She softened, "OK, you buy me drink now."

I looked over at Billy. "Wipe that shit-eatin' grin off and let's have some more drinks then we'll go eat," I said.

"What about the boat?" he asked.

"That's the way the cookie crumbles. Let's get FUUUU-CKED UP..."

❧

The three of us walked across the street to a little cantina, a hole-in-the-wall type of place; with one long, greasy table covered with oilcloth and two benches. An old woman stood bent over a portable hot-table with a small grill as steam rose into her pores. She fixed us huevos rancheros, and brought over three beers. While I was waiting, I picked up my bottle and stepped out on the boardwalk to watch Boys Town at ten in the morning. At that time of day it should have been called Girls Town. All I could see were women, up and down the street, young, middle-aged, old ones, and real old ones. Most of them had been in the business at one time or another. Couples walking around, some drinking like us, but most of the girls were on daily errands. Getting their hair done, shopping, with kids in tow. The daily routine of any small town.

I had just sat down and started eating my eggs when Theresa, Billy's girl from the night before, came through the door. She walked over and ordered a tequila straight. She took the little glass and shot it down then ordered another one. Billy watched her as she stomped over to the table, hands on hips, "Where you been, I look all over this town for you?"

Billy looked up at her with that shy smile of his, "We were at the El Paso till just a while ago, then came over here to get some food," he said.

"I wait for you, I want to make love with you one more time, you no come back," Theresa said, tapping her foot.

"Well, I ran into Pat here, and then Maria showed up so we decided to eat before we got too drunk. Do you want something to go with that tequila?" he asked, tipping the beer to his lips.

"Yes! You get me mad. Pay for my drinks. I have no money." She sat down with folded arms, "One of these days I cut you balls off, then you see."

Even mad theresa was a beautiful girl. She seemed to be play-acting. She was all of seventeen and in love with Billy. Maria pulled her chair in close to mine, grabbing my arm with one hand and my shirt with the other, "You pay attention to me now!" She stood up and ordered a round of tequila for everybody, then kicked my foot and said, "You pay."

I pulled out a bunch of bills, tossing them on the table. I looked over at Billy and he winked one eye and a nod of the head.

After we finished eating I ordered more beer. I didn't want to get too drunk too fast. The day was still young, and I'd never make it till dark at this rate. But, Theresa ordered more tequila. I wondered where in hell she put it. It didn't seem to affect her at all. Several drinks later Maria punched my shoulder and said, "We go now." She stood up and headed for the door. I followed her out and down the street.

We were heading west, walking toward the San Luis club, but were on the wrong side of the street. I thought she might be taking me to her room, but she kept stopping and talking to almost everyone we met. Finally, she took my hand and playfully pulled me across the street, I knew this was it, we were going to make it together. I sure was glad we drank as much as we did because I would have been like a rabbit if I hadn't. This would be my first time since leaving Ohio.

We entered the building from the west side near the back. The hall was pitch black after the bright sunlight. When my eyes focused, I saw Maria's white blouse briefly as she turn into a doorway, I followed her in. Maria stood in the center of the room, looking at me with sensual eyes. I closed the door behind me and moved toward her. She unbuttoned her blouse one button at a time, never taking her eyes off mine. She reached around and unsnapped her bra. The blouse and bra slipped to the floor and the most beautiful set of breasts stood out looking at me. My knees got weak, I could feel the ache in my thighs and thought, I have to be able to please her, or this will be over in a flash; she goes to bed with seven or eight guys every night. I stopped thinking. The skirt crumpled to the floor. Maria rolled her panties down slowly. My heart was racing, my throat went all dry, as I stood there frozen. She walked over to the bed and lay down, her eyes still on me. She raised her arms for me to fill. Slowly, be slow, I kept telling myself. I tripped over my left foot, stumbled over to the bed and sat down beside her. My eyes caressed the nipples of her breasts as my hand began rubbing her thighs. Then her nipples, all of a sudden, were between my lips. My emotions starting to cascade in on me; my mind kept saying, "Slowly, slowly."

∾

I awoke to voices. Maria was talking to a young girl about ten years old. I rubbed my eyes as I looked at the girl; she gave me a big smile, and said "Una cerveza?" Maria nodded, and looked at my reflection in the mirror as she put on makeup. She sat at the vanity, nude. It was then I realized I was nude too, lying there on the bed. The girl took it in stride; what was one more nude male? Well, it was something to me. I pulled a sheet up over my waist.

"You're awake, mi amour," she said."

"Mi amour?" I repeated.

"My love, you're my lovely one."

"Then you liked the way I made love to you?" I said, sitting up with my hands behind my head.

"You did real good, mi amour, I want you to come back tonight. Will you be around?"

"Come on over here, why wait till tonight? How do you say, turn off the light? And close the door in Spanish?"

She stood up, and ran over and dove onto the bed, "Avoca la loose, seta la porta. Avoca la loose, turn off the light. Seta la porta, close the door. Now don't mess up my makeup, I have to go to work in a while."

"Ah, you like me a little?" I asked.

She reached down and grabbed my erection that propped up the sheet, "I like you a lot, mi amour, you're a good boy."

"A good boy, me muy macho…"

"Una cerveza," I heard a voice say. I looked over to see the little girl holding a bottle of beer.

"For me?" I asked.

"Si, senor," she said. I took the bottle and looked at Maria.

"I knew you'd want one when you woke," she said.

I reached for my pants to get some money.

"I got it already, you my man now!" as she waved the girl off. She squeezed my erection. It had started to fade, but was on the rise again now that the girl had left.

❧

Later Maria stood in the center of the room with her evening dress on and asked,

"How I look, mi amour?"

"You look great, baby." She gave me a big smile.

I was lying there nude, when in pops one of the girls from down the hall; she gave me a big smile as she sized me up. It was too late to grab a sheet. What the hell, the room was becoming more like a train station all the time. The girl shot off a bunch of Spanish, faster then I could keep up. Maria rattled it off right back at her then said to me, "Here is a key for this room when you come back tonight. Don't drink in the bar tonight when I work, and don't mess with other girls. I find out if you do, all hell break loose. If you want a bath you find it down the hall." She came over and gave me a kiss.

I started to object, but, said, "OK." She left me there sipping on the warm beer. "I am a Pa-ro-ta, a Pimp, a great lover," I thought. I lay there a while, thinking and drinking, then decided to see if they had a shower around someplace. I put my pants on and stepped out into the hall. A couple of girls were walking towards the bar. "Buenos noches," one of them said.

"How you girls doing?" I said, feeling more at home all the time. Down the hall was like ten feet, then I found myself in a U-shaped courtyard. I looked around confused, then saw a doorway across the yard. A walkway went around the building. I followed the path to a doorway, and sure enough found the showers. Five shower heads lined up against the wall, no stalls. I went back to the room to get my clothes, and on the way I ran into the young girl who had brought the beer earlier. "Ah Senorita, Yo tango una cerveza, por favor. OK?"

"OK, una cerveza," she said."

I keep talking like this I'll be speaking fluent Spanish in no time. I gave her a dollar and told her to put the beer in the room, I'd get it later.

I found a bar of soap and a towel and returned to the shower. The shower room was ten by ten and all tile, cold as hell. I had started washing my hair when two girls walked in. They looked at me a second and giggled, then took off their clothes and got right in there with me. I stood there, wondering what to do. Hell, if it was all right with them, it was all right with me. What more could a guy ask for then two little beauties in the same shower.

"Donde Maria?" one of them asked

"Working," I said, "Word sure gets around fast." They giggled again. "I guess if I want to keep my balls I'd better get out of here. I'll see you girls later." I toweled off my hair and put my pants back on; then left, the girls laughing behind me.

The beer was waiting in the room when I got there. I sat thinking about the shower and what to do now. Maybe Billy was out and about or one of the other guys. "I guess I'll go see what's happening on the street," I said aloud, pushing myself up off the bed.

Didn't Look Back

CHAPTER SIX

Perfect Dawn

I got back to Port Isabel before noon. I stopped in at a Mexican cantina a block or so from the docks, for a quick beer to shake my hangover. The October sky foretold rain with its gathering of clouds.

"Que Paso, Mamasita?" I asked. She was a big, heavy woman sitting on a bar stool at the end of the bar. She grabbed a towel and ran it over the bar on her way down to where I sat. "How you do?" she asked.

"Good, I'll have a glass of beer," I said. "Kind of quiet in here today?"

"Most everybody fishing, I guess," she put the glass under the tap at an angle while it slowly filled.

I sat and sipped the beer, thinking about Boys Town.

"Where you been?"

I turned around to see Rocky coming through the side door. His hat was on the back of his head and he was wearing his fishing boots, rolled down just below the knee.

"I just got back from Boys Town."

"I thought maybe you left town. You missed your boat, didn't you?"

"Yeah, I missed it. I heard you went to jail the other night."

"They got me! What can I say; you have anything to do with that?" He walked over to the bar a couple stools away from me and stood watching me.

"Hell no, I passed out in Maria Lana's room. I didn't hear anything about it 'til the next morning."

"Yeah, I heard you were back there." He paused a minute… "What are you up to now?"

"I guess I'll try to find a boat" I said.

"Well, if you want a job, get your gear and be over at the ice house in an hour." He turned and left.

What the hell's he up to, I wondered. Is he thinking of tossing me over the side when we get out? Everybody knew we had a fight the other night. I sat wondering about the conversation, and Boys Town. The hell with it. I went after my gear.

ᴄᴈ

The ice house was the last building on the docks at the end. My gear was in the fish house. After retrieving it I headed south toward the *Perfect Dawn,* the bag over my shoulder. The excitement was starting to well up inside as I thought about the job with Rocky. He was one of the best fishermen in the fleet. I could learn a lot from him if I put my head to it. As I approached the two-story metal building, I could see a chute coming out the side of the building; a big black hose one foot thick hung down over the boat. The ice came out the chute and down the hose, into the hold of the boat.

I walked up to the boat, a seventy-foot, black, steel-hulled boat, the white cabin taking up a third of the foredeck. Big four-by-ten wooden doors were lying against the rails. The doors were reinforced with steel so that when they opened the nets and sank to the bottom they'd stay there. There were two doors to each net, one on each side of the opening. The nets were sprawled around the back deck, the big hatch cover lay ajar. I stepped up on the boat and peered down into the hole. I could see Wedo's blond head bobbing up and down, swearing to himself.

"Hey Wedo, mind if I get in on the conversation?" I asked.

Fifteen or twenty baskets were stacked upon each other around the hatch. I grabbed the first stack and moved it over so as to get at the ladder. Wedo looked up at me with wild, greenish-blue eyes, his mustache hanging down the sides of his mouth, the blond hair down to his shoulders… recognition, then the smile.

"You got here, huh? I didn't think you'd show," he said, grabbing onto the ladder.

"Well, what the hell, either I go swimming or I go to work." I straightened up as he climbed out of the hold.

"Rocky said you had balls, he also said you'd be here; so you can help me ice up. Get your self a coat and a pair of gloves up there in the cabin," he pointed someplace up forward. "I have to go call that grocer and get his ass on the stick or we won't eat." He jumped off the boat and headed up the dock.

The boat was tied to the port side, bow facing south. I walked around the cabin to my left until I came to a door and went inside. A table bolted up against the wall on the port side, a four-burner stove next to the sink on the starboard side. To my right three steps going down led to a room with four bunks; each bunk had two drawers for clothes. I threw my bag up on a top bunk and went back to the main part of the cabin. Rain gear hung by the door, I found a jacket and gloves; then went to the wheel house in the front of the cabin. The wheel house had its own door with windows all around. The pilothouse was about ten-foot wide with a five foot depth. The wheel and a big leather chair occupied in the center; a compass mounted on the shelf sat in front of the wheel. A huge depth sounder hung on the back wall, with a paper read out. Under the shelf was a handle I assumed was the auto-pilot. I was trying to get a feel for the boat so as not to look stupid when asked to do something. I headed back to the fish hold.

Wedo was rearranging the baskets when I came around the corner. A two-inch water hose hung over the edge of the hatch.

"What-cha need?" I asked.

"Hit the water," he said, climbing down the ladder.

I jumped out to the dock and turned on the water. I got back on the boat and peered down into the hole; it was one big room split into eight sections with one-by-six boards, two in front, two on the sides and two in back. Wedo was splashing water all over the place, then funneling it to a big eight inch drain in the center of the floor. After he finished I turned off the water. Wedo came up the ladder and stepped out. "You ever ice up?" He took off the gloves and started moving the big black ice hose over the hatch opening.

"I've watched it being done," I stood there looking at him as I put on my gloves.

"Well, it's your time, Cap'n, get your ass down there and get to ice'n," he said with a mischievous smile.

I climbed down into the hole and looked around. Each room was five by six and seven foot high. I put four boards in all the doorways. The big hose came down the hole, it had a three-foot rope tied around the end.

"Grab the rope with one hand, put your arm around the hose, and aim," he said.

"Ready," I yelled.

I could hear the ice coming down the chute, but I wasn't as ready as I

79

thought. It was as if a big black snake came alive in my hands. It lifted me right off the deck! After what seemed an eternity I finally got it under control. I iced up to the top board and moved to next room. The ice stopped coming down after the third room, I looked up…

"We're just gonna do three, so go ahead and put in all but the last two boards," Wedo said, peering down at me. I put in the boards, then looked up at Wedo and said, "I'm freezing my balls off down here." I danced around reaching for a cigarette. "Let me get this smoke lit."

"Let's get to humpin', my man, and make sure you get those corners good."

I could hear the ice coming down as I quickly lit the cigarette; I threw the match in the air and grabbed onto the hose. "That dirty fucker," I yelled into the roar of the ice as it came out like gangbusters. It felt good to the ears when the ice stopped. My hands were like little ice cubes. I jumped for the ladder and climbed out as fast as I could. Up on deck I was stomping my feet while putting my hands in my armpits. "Whew! That's colder then a well-digger's ass."

"If you liked that job just wait till we go to Mexico. The whole hold gets filled with ice right up to the hatch cover. You ever been down to old Mexico fishing?" he asked, motioning to the operator with his hand to take the hose away.

"You mean way down in Mexico? Naw, I never been down there. Mick was talking about Vera Cruz the other day. Is that where you're talking about?"

"Yep, that's the place. If you hang around long enough we'll be heading down that way in about two months. Just fuckin' and fishin', that's all we do down there." He grabbed three or four baskets and dropped them down into the hold.

"Fuckin' and fishin' huh, sounds like the place I might like to be. You think Rocky will want to take me along?" I handed Wedo four more baskets to drop in the hold.

"Sure! We'll need a three-man crew, just to keep our insurance. Shit man, you'll love it down there. They bring the women and booze out in bum boats.

"What's a bum boat?" I asked.

"A fifteen to twenty foot boat, with a wide beam for hauling cargo. There is this island off Vera Cruz we call Pie Island. We just drop the hook and it all comes to us. We'll be down there about two months or so. It's a ball, man, and you make a lot money. No place to spend it."

"I'm convinced, let's go today," I said.

"I'll tell you what, we'll put the groceries on ice and clean up the back deck, then go have a beer till Rocky gets here.

❧

My hands were still stinging when I turned off the water to the hose. I looked up and there stood Rocky on the dock with his rubber boots in hand. So much for the beer.

"Are you guys ready to rock and roll?" Rocky asked, as he grabbed the rail and jumped aboard.

"We're in'em, Cap'n," Wedo said.

"Get those engines started, you should-a had' em purring by now." Rocky looked back over at me and said, "You ready to catch some fish?"

"You bet," I said, pulling a cigarette out of my pocket. "I was just wondering how serious you were about the job," I lit the smoke and inhaled.

"You need a job and I need a header. The insurance companies won't insure a two-man crew anymore, so we have to have a third man, it's a company thing." Rocky started to turn, then said, "If you're worried about getting your ass kicked the other night, don't. I love to fight. It's almost as good as sex. Besides I don't hold a grudge."

"I was a little concerned," I said nodding my head, taking a quick drag on the smoke. "You get in a fight one night and a couple of days later the same guy offers you a job."

"That's the way it is working these boats. If you don't fight, the fishermen'll think you're a pussy. You took a couple of good hits the other night. I liked that; don't be afraid to fight around here. You'll get work faster with your ass kicked than if you chicken out. Just do a good job and you'll be OK," Rocky said, disappearing into the cabin.

Fifteen minutes later the boat was moving down the channel. I was standing on the back deck watching the buildings move away behind us. Several seagulls flew overhead. The clouds were still crunching in on each other, big and dark. Rain for sure, I thought. I saw sandy beach off to the sides, and brush in the background, as we motored out.

"Let's get those outriggers down," Wedo said, as he came around the port side of the cabin.

He moved over to a big winch up close to the cabin. I watched Wedo bring a line over from the rail and tie it off on the winch-head. Two heads moving in opposite directions. I went over and grabbed the second line from the starboard rail and tied it off on the other head, and slowly let the pole down. Wedo got hold of the handles on the winch and brought the cables in till they were taut. He took a small line and tied the brake down, then headed forward to the pilot house.

I checked the back deck for anything that might wash over the side and made sure it was all tied down. I looked up to see a sailboat being pushed down the channel by the wind. It's mainsail all the way out. I stood day-dreaming about myself at the helm of a sailboat when Wedo came out on deck and said, "We'll drop the nets around eight, so you might wanta get some sleep till then."

"Later," I said.

When we came out of the jetty; an ocean swell began rocking the boat back and forth. To the east I could see Padre Island. One other shrimper was steaming in from the south. I was too excited to sleep. We were headed in a southwesterly direction, the wind hitting on the starboard side of the boat. I moved to the port side and forward as far as I could and still be out of the wind. I put my head in close to the cabin and pulled up the collar on my jacket to light a cigarette. I inhaled deeply and felt the rhythm of the boat under my feet. I stepped forward to the window and waved at Rocky to let him know I was still out on deck. Then I was back against the cabin in my own little world, thinking about the money I could make down in Mexico. A lot of things went through my head. Boys Town, California, and then I saw the porpoises. There must have been twenty or so swimming alongside the boat on both sides and in front. I watched them race along the side for fifteen minutes, then they were gone as fast as they came. Seagulls flew along behind us. As I watched them, a monster bird landed on the cross-tree of the mast. He was the biggest bird I'd ever seen. The only name I could come up with was a California condor. The bird was over four feet high. His wing spread eight feet across. His beak extended out from the head four inches and made a sharp downward turn of an inch or so. He just got tired of fly-ing I guess and thought he'd hitch a ride. A light rain was coming down as I walked up to the bow, waves crashing against the side of the hull. I could feel a surge of life go through me; it felt great to be alive. I walked back toward the cabin, looking up to see if the bird was still there. He was.

The cabin was warm and the coffee was on. Rocky was in the pilothouse. I stuck my head in and asked if he wanted any coffee, "Yeah, make it black

82

with two sugars." I poured two cups and took one up to Rocky, "How long before we get there?" I asked.

"Three or four hours yet, you should get some sleep. You never know what might happen. You could be up the rest of the night."

"I'll lie down after I drink my coffee."

One red light was burning in the wheelhouse for night vision, and the instruments were lit up. Rocky sat in semi-darkness, talking into the microphone to one of the shrimpers.

I set the cup down in front of him and went back out to the main cabin. I stepped down and got a book from my bag. When Les got out of jail, he gave me a list of books to read, "You'll be pretty well read if you read these books," he'd said. I pulled out the "Catcher in the Rye," by J.D. Salinger. I laid down on one a top bunk and turned on the little light, rolling with the rhythm of the boat. Wedo was asleep in the bottom bunk across from me.

"Hit the deck! It's time to drop'em!"

Somebody was shaking me. I awoke wondering where in hell I was; looking around, it came back. I jumped down on the deck, tugged on my rubber boots, and grabbed a rain jacket. I stepped up into the main cabin. Wedo was pouring coffee, "It'll be fifteen minutes or so till we drop 'em so you might as well have a cup."

"Thanks, man, did I sleep hard," I said, stretching my back and scratching my head with both hands. I picked up the cup and sat down to gather my wits. Wedo went up front to talk to Rocky.

I was sitting, smoking a cigarette and drinking coffee when Wedo came walking quickly back, "Let's go."

I took one last drink and followed him out.

Rocky was turning the boat into the wind as I stepped out. The rain and wind hit full on and I made my way to the back deck. Wedo stood there, hair flying, motioning for me to come over, 'Whatever you do, don't step on the net. When I get the doors over, make sure everything goes over smoothly, and pay attention to the lazy line. Last week a guy stepped on one and went down with the nets. No way to get you back in this weather. That guy didn't make it either."

Wedo went up to the winch, pulled the ropes off the brake handles and put his toes on the brake pedals. I went over and untied the big doors, then staggered out to the center of the deck, making sure nothing was in the way. Wedo took up a little cable, testing it, then with a roar the doors left the deck, stopping just short of the boom. He did the starboard side, then the port. The nets had been flaked along the rail, they now followed along with the doors, the lazy line uncoiled from the deck. The doors rocked back and forth as the nets streamed out forty feet along each side. Wind, rain, and waves smashed up against the boat; made a person wonder how you could get the doors and nets down without tangling the whole rig up.

In the pilot house, Rocky put the throttle all the way forward (in the corner, as they say). As Wedo let the cable out slowly, the big doors crashed into the water and the nets spread out and sunk down into the depths. The lazy line runs full-length along the outside of the nets, running free. I checked to see that everything was loose and free. When we brought the nets back up I got a long pole with a hook on it, reached out and grabbed the lazy line, took it over and wrapped it around the wench head in order to have control of the net. The nets drag along the bottom above the mud. The tickler chain drags a little below the net, tickling the noses of the shrimp. They will jump up and be scooped into the net.

Wedo jammed the handles into the gears of the winch, tied them off, and came over to where I stood. "See that big-assed bird up there? I wonder how long he's been up there."

"He landed within the first half hour after we left," I said, looking up at the bird.

"That son's-a-bitch," he said pointing at the bird, "He ain't s'posed to be there, and I don't want him there."

"Hey, man, he's a great looking bird; he just needs a rest from it all. He'll be gone in a couple of hours," I said trying to calm Wedo down. I couldn't believe he got so excited about the bird. "Let's go have a cup of coffee," I said.

"Coffee hell, I'm going back to bed, up in three hours. You better get some sleep too."

"OK. I'll do it, right after I have a cup."

⚘

I got my pole and latched onto the lazy line, winching the bulging foot of the net over to the side of the boat. In the meantime, Wedo had a rope ready and slipped it around the net. The rope ran through a block on the boom fifteen feet in the air, then back to the winch. Wedo followed the rope back and started winching up the net. I let go the lazy line and with the net in the air, I pushed-pulled the full bag over to the center of the deck and kept it a foot off the deck. A skirt of thick webbing circled the bulging sack. I lifted the skirt and grabbed one end of the slip-knot and pulled. Out slammed a thousand pounds of every kind of fish imaginable, plus several kinds unknown to me. The pile was two feet high and spread all over the deck. I quickly retied the knot and the nets were back on their way to the bottom.

I spotted two sand sharks, two and three feet long. I grabbed their tails and threw them over the side. Had I left them on deck, they'd be dead in no time. I got the little stool, my rake and started sorting out the shrimp, tearing off the heads as I went. We got a hundred and forty pounds of shrimp off that drag. The rest of the fish, crabs, and what have you was considered garbage and it all went back over the side, dead or dying. About eight hundred pounds of fish; what a waste, but there was nothing I could do about it.

Our two big flood lights lit up the back deck and twenty feet out on either side of the boat. As I pushed the trash off the boat through the scupper holes, the water came alive; all you could see were the backs of sharks. Ten and twelve foot sharks as far as the eye could see!

"I'm going to catch me one of those big bastards if it's the last thing I do," Wedo said, then took off up front someplace. I went over and sat on the back rail. A steel cable, the back stay, ran up to the mast. I leaned against it. Wedo came back with a big spike nail, hammer, and pliers, then bent the nail in a V shape and tied it to the end of a line with a good sized fish for bait. The other end he tied to the stay I'd been leaning against. I moved over a little and for the next few minutes watched him try to catch a shark. I didn't notice that I was between the rope and the back of the boat. A couple of times Wedo almost had one, but they all got away.

I was casually sitting there, when this thought started in through the right side of my head and passed behind my eyes, I stopped it. "What if a shark got a hold of that line and took off toward the back of the boat?" I thought about that a second, then reached down, and grabbed the rail and started up. At the same instant the rope hit me hard in the gut. I got my feet on the deck while pushing the line away with one hand and pulling on the stay with the other. It was all I could do to hang on. "Wedo, give me a hand here!" I yelled.

Wedo was jumping up and down with glee that he had caught a shark. He looked back at me, then took two steps, drawing his knife as he came; he cut the rope, "What the hell you doing getting caught up in my fishing line! Now I'll have to catch another one."

"Thanks. That wasn't anything I tried to do on purpose." But for a split second I was almost shark bait. Wedo was totally unaware of my predicament. He was jumping up and down with joy over catching a shark. The close call scared the hell out of me, and I wondered just where that thought had come from, It had saved my life.

After we picked up the last drag we headed inshore to anchor for the day. Wedo fixed breakfast: bacon, eggs, grits, toast, and lots of coffee. It was after seven in the morning and my eyes were still stinging from lack of sleep and salt water. Not a cloud in the sky, the ocean a deep blue, the boat rocking to the waves. I finished my third cup of coffee and did the dishes. Rocky and Wedo crawled into their bunks to sleep for the day. I got my book, cigarettes, another cup of coffee, then went out on the back deck. I couldn't just let this beautiful day go by sleeping. The bird was still in the cross-tree of the mast. I looked up at him and said, "Good morning, Mr. Bird. How are you this morning?" His dispassionate look told me he didn't want to be disturbed. I looked out over the water and found it too hard to resist. I took off my clothes and jumped off the stern of the boat for a swim. After a few minutes I thought about the sharks of the night before. With Rocky and Wedo sleeping, all of a sudden this didn't seem like such a good idea. I swam to the back of the boat. It was too high to get a hand up. I swam around to the side where the outriggers came down. I was able to grab a chain hanging off and with imaginary sharks coming after me I pulled myself up and over the side and stood there laughing, the fear inside me subsiding. I looked out over the water, nothing. I went back and got a hot cup of coffee. Next time I'd stay in a little longer. I just have to overcome my fear. I lit a cigarette and sat down with the book thinking, this is the life.

༒

We had weighed anchor and were headed offshore to drop the nets. I was coiling the line when Wedo came out of the cabin with a twenty-two rifle and headed for the back deck. "What's up!" I yelled over the waves and engine, but he kept going without saying a word. I felt I knew what he had in mind. When I got to the back deck he had the rifle aimed in the air, and I heard the shot. When I came to a stop and looked up the bird just sat there, then pitched forward and dropped to the deck. For a second I thought he had killed it, but the bird just sat there shaking its head, looking confused. His eyes seemed to focus, and you could tell this was a mad bird. He let out a beller and was up and running, striking at the first thing that got in his way which happened to be Wedo; who started running toward me, laughing. I made for the cabin door. Wedo was right on my tail as I went through the door and shut it. The bird on the other side, "Man is he pissed off or what," I said, laughing so hard that Rocky stepped in from the pilot house.

"What in hell's happening with you guys?"

"Wedo just got nipped by that bird out there," I said.

"The son's-a-bitch nailed me right in the ass," Wedo moaned. He had a pained look on his face.

"Pat, take a look at his ass and see if his brains are falling out," Rocky said, and stepped into the pilot house closing the door.

"Well, pull 'em down and let's have a look," I said. Wedo let his pants slide down. "You better lie over the table so I can fix this, he got you pretty good." I grabbed a clean rag and wiped the blood away. "Believe it or not there's not that much blood." Wedo had a one-inch gash in his buttocks. I poured iodine all over it, then squeezed the lips together and taped it with band-aids. "You should have stitches in it I guess, but this'll work or I'll always think it should have."

Wedo pulled up his pants and went over to the door and looked out the window. "You think he's gone yet? Maybe we should have a cup of coffee before we go check," Wedo said, with both hands on the window.

A while later I stepped out on the deck looking both ways, not seeing the bird I walked slowly to the back looking around carefully, no bird. He was gone, never to be seen again.

❧

Two nights later, Wedo was bringing in the tri-net, which is a small net run off the side of the boat. It is a tenth the size of the big nets; we drag it for a short period of time in order to get an average of how much shrimp is on the bottom. As the tri-net broke the surface I saw something big, but couldn't tell what it was. We got a line around it and hauled the net up on deck. I was back by the wench when Wedo pulled the cord on the net. An enormous sea turtle landed on the deck.

He had a massive head, ten inches wide, and his shell was two and a half feet across. When he opened his mouth I stepped back a few feet thinking, if he ever got that mouth around your leg, he'd never let go. In the meantime Wedo jumped around to his side and flipped the turtle over onto his back. Before I could say a word, Wedo reached down with the knife and cut the turtle's throat. When he hit the jugular, blood squirted out fifteen feet. Wedo looked like something out of a bizarre movie, "What the hell'd you do that for? We could'a thrown him back," I said.

"Man, haven't you ever had salt water turtle? It'll be the best stuff you ever ate," Wedo said, and started in cutting up the turtle.

I got to admit that when he cooked up a roast the next night, it was some of the best meat that I had ever eaten.

A few nights later, after midnight, we had just picked up the second drag. I stood on the back deck, rain pelting my face. Wedo was on the wench. The boat rolled sideways and a gust of wind hit, knocking me off balance. I skated to the rail, hitting it hard, letting out a yell. I grabbed a stay and came to a quick stop. I was bent over the rail looking down into water, "Woo-ee look at all those fucking sharks, this is no time to be swimming," I yelled.

"Quit fucking around, will ya, get that line around the net."

Rain gear is bulky and it's hard to move quickly in it. Everything slows down and you work twice as hard. I got a line around the net and Wedo winched it in. Rocky came out on deck and yelled, "Bring it all in and put it on deck. The sharks have been eating the shit out of it. We're gonna have to sew up the holes."

For the next hour Wedo and Rocky sewed on the nets. I headed the shrimp, getting them ready to be iced down. Finally Rocky said, "That's enough. Let's get them back in the water. Wedo, take the wheel and when you get her into the wind, put the balls to the wall. I want those doors to go straight to the bottom before the sharks can get to 'em."

I got the nets flaked on the rail and the lazy line ready to run, then looked out into the rainy night, "Jesus Katie Keehrist, look at all those lights." I yelled. We were converging on the whole fleet it seemed. There must have been forty boats ahead of us.

"Then they'll have to fucking move," Rocky yelled, as the boat came into the wind. The wind ripped through the rigging. The rain coming down sideways; the nose of the boat went under a wave and the deck became a torrent of water. I could feel the vibration of the engines under my feet as Wedo gave her full throttle. The noise was deafening and my heart was pounding with excitement. The doors disappeared under the water, the cables were running and then something happened. The boat turned and the engines slowed. I looked out over the water, the lights that were in front of us were now off to the left. Rocky let out a primal scream while locking the winch, then ran forward.

The engines came alive again. A scared and confused Wedo came back on deck. He nervously let out the cables. I went to the stern and watched the cables; they didn't look right. As I stood there, Rocky came up behind me. When I noticed him I got out of his way. He had a terrible look on his face. For a second I thought Rocky might pitch me over the side. It took a minute, then he lost it; he started stomping all over, shaking his fist at the air, at Wedo, then at me. He seemed to be mad at the gods and all mankind for giving him the most miserable crew on earth. I even heard a few words I'd never heard before. As quick as it started it was over. Rocky threw up his arms and said, "Well, it's a tangled mess and you two are going to untangle it, no matter what it takes." He stomped up to the wheelhouse and cut the engines.

It was four in the morning before we got the doors and nets on board. Rocky was good to his word, he went to bed. I went in and made a pot of coffee. It was going to be a long day.

CHAPTER SEVEN

Meeting Old Friends

It was two o'clock in the afternoon when I jumped off the *Perfect Dawn* to tie the bow line. Wedo took care of the stern line. I was all excited about going to Boys Town. I stood up, turned around, and there was Jim with a big smile on his ruddy face.

"So you went to work for Rocky, huh? I kind of wondered if you'd get down this way," he said, stretching his hand out.

"Shit, man, is it good to see you or what," I said, grabbing his hand and giving it a shake. "Are you going to be around for a couple of days? I still owe you twenty from that wild night in Freeport. I thought I was a gonner when they through me in jail, but it all seems to work itself out. Tell you what, I'll get cleaned up a little and we can hit the town."

Rocky stepped out of the wheel house and grabbed the rail with both hands, "What the hell you doing down in this neck of the woods Jim, lose your way or did you just decide to come down to God's country?"

"Hey, Rocky, long time no see, I heard you were making money hand over fist, so I thought I'd come down and relieve you of some of it." Jim pulled a smoke out of his pocket and stuck it between his lips, "Ol' Cap'n Jack went on a bender a week ago Tuesday. Haven't seen hide nor hair of him since." He lit the cigarette, "We just been tied to the dock for bout eight days now."

"No shit!" Rocky said, putting a leg over the rail and jumping down to the dock, "I'd bet top dollar that old muff diver's hauled ass down to old Mexico, and one of them whores got hold him and jus won't let go."

"Naw, the sons-a-bitch just hauled ass period. I went over to Boys Town and no sign of him; I looked all over Matamoras and Brownsville, nobody has seen him since the first day we got here."

Wedo came over and stood by me, listening.

"Never fear, that ol' bastard'll show up," Rocky said.

"Well, to be totally honest about it, I don't gave a shit if he shows or not. A lawyer down in Houston owns the Linda Lu; he told me I could take her over tomorrow, if Jack don't show, so now I'm looking for a rig-man. You happen to know a good man?"

Rocky scratched the back of his head, pushing his cap forwards, "Not right off the top." Rocky gave Jim a quick look, "Don't be fucking with my crew, either, sombody'll show in the next day or so. In the meanwhile, we should celebrate. Let's go up town and get shit-faced, then we'll head over to Boys' Town and get us a couple gals and do it up right… come to think of it though, I should let you have that blond headed bastard over there. He's the worst rig man I ever had. Well, I can't really say that, but he sure is the stupidest."

Rocky looked at me and said, "Go up to the store and get yourself a six-pack, then come back and unload the shrimp and clean the boat. I don't want to see either one of you in a bar till everything is done, or I'll be kicking ass if I do."

Wedo jumped up on the boat and grabbed the hatch cover and lifted it up; it dropped, and he got it up again. This time the cover came off. I knew he was cussing under his breath. I had gotten to know Wedo pretty good after this last trip. Wedo would do anything to make up for his stupidity, except stand up for himself.

I kept thinking, say something, goddamit!

Jim just stood there not saying anything.

"You know what these two fuckers did to me?" Rocky said to Jim.

"Hold on now, I didn't have a thing to do with those doors flipping," I said.

"Doors flipping?" Jim said, and started laughing.

"Jim, you ain't heard the worst yet," Rocky said, and gave me a dirty look and said "You're part of the crew right?"

"Yeah," I said.

"Then you share in the responsibility, no matter what happens, and don't give me any shit, I'm still pissed off enough to kick ass." Rocky took hold of Jim's arm, turning him around, and they started up the dock, "Anyway, I was up to my ass in sharks, they were eating us alive. I had to get the nets up fast and down quickly. I put Wedo on the wheel and I took the winch. Things were going along pretty good till I started to drop them. Wedo out of nowhere makes a right turn and the doors flip, the whole rig gets tangled, and it takes twenty-four hours to undo that mess…

"Or I'll be kicking ass," I heard Wedo mimic. I looked up and Wedo was marching back and forth, hands in the air, "Or I'll be kicking ass," he repeated, walking over to the rail, looking down at me, shaking his fist. "That wasn't my goddamn fault. If that boat hadn't moved in our way I wouldn't a had to make that turn."

"Hey man, I believe ya, you just have to convince Rocky," I said.

"He's going to ruin my reputation if he keeps telling that story. Nobody will hire me."

"I wouldn't worry about it, Rocky's not going to let anybody hire you anyway. He's got you so afraid to make a move, there's no way you'll ever quit."

He gave me a dirty look, and gave me the finger, "Fuck you," he said.

I laughed, "Anything else you want? I'm going after that beer."

"Naw, just get the beer and be quick about it. I want to head into town as soon as possible."

At the store I got the beer, some cigarettes, and a couple hamburgers with fries. I was on a street parallel to the docks. I looked over to see crazy Dave standing two hundred feet from me. I hadn't seen that bawd head since Freeport. "Hey Dave," I yelled, waving an arm. He just stood there looking at me, then turned and ran toward the docks and around a building. I stood there wandering what the hell.

Wedo was lowering a fish box down into the hole with a one-arm crane that had been pushed out over the boat. He saw me and came over to get a beer and burger. "The strangest thing just happened, I said. You know Crazy Dave, don't you? He's on the *Vagabond*."

"Yeah, I know him from last year. He's a weird guy, I'll tell you that," Wedo said.

"Well I met him up in Freeport a couple of months ago. Jim, Dave, and I went out on the town together, had a pretty good time till I got thrown in jail. Anyway, I just saw him so I called out, and waved. He looked at me as if he didn't know me, then ran away. Strangest thing I ever saw."

"Like I said, he's a weird guy," Wedo said, biting into his burger. "He's paranoid half the time."

"Paranoid! What's that mean?"

"You smoke dope and don't know what paranoid means. You sure as hell will find out one of these days. It means somebody is after you all the time, even when there's no one there. It's just in your head."

"What's that got to do with smoking pot?" I asked, pulling out a beer.

"It just goes with the turf, you'll see. Let's get this goddamn boat unloaded and head up to the bar. Jump down into the hole and start loading those baskets. I'll work the crane." Wedo stood and threw the beer bottle over the side, then grabbed the hose and said, "Hit the water first. I'll hose down the back deck till you get everything ready."

∞

The sun was just going down when I came out of the shower. The sky was a brilliant red. The wind had laid down and the bay was still as glass. Everything was quiet. A couple of fishermen stood on the dock, talking two hundred feet away. There must have been thirty or forty boats tied up along the wharf. Wedo was leaning against a building smoking a cigarette. "What in hell took you so long?" he asked, stepping on the butt of his cigarette. I ran over and threw my dirty clothes on the boat and came back.

"Have to make my ass pretty in case I run into that woman."

"What woman?"

"The one we're all looking for. Let's go," I said. We started up the street. We had just got past the end of a row of company buildings, an empty field sat vacant before the next set of buildings started. Two loud blasts went off like a shotgun, real close by. Wedo and I almost jumped out of our skin, "Where the fuck did that come from?" Wedo yelled.

"I don't know, but let's get the hell out of here; that was too close for comfort."

We ran, bent low, to the first building. Two more shots went off as we got behind the building. "You OK?" I asked. We leaned in tight to the building. Wedo stuck his head out and looked around the corner, "Shit, man! It's that asshole Dave. He thinks he owns the whole goddamn country. Take a look at this asshole."

I peeked around the corner to see Dave walking up and down the dock, rifle at the ready and not a stitch on. He was bare ass naked. "What ya thinks the matter with him?" I asked.

"Damn if I know, but I ain't dealing with his shit. I'm going up to get a drink."

94

"I'm gonna see what's going on with his ass," I said, stepping out from behind the building. Dave was still walking back and forth yelling, "I know you fuckers are out there, and I'm not giving up. I'll take half you bastards with me. Come on, come on, let's get it on!"

"Hey Dave, what's the deal? It's me, Pat." Two more shots. I jumped back behind the building. "Thank God he's shooting in the air," I said. "Maybe we should go and have that beer after all."

"My sentiments exactly," Wedo said.

C/3

Johnny Cash was singing, "I Walk the Line" when we came through the door. The bar was to our right with five men sitting along it, with a big, dark complexioned guy serving drinks. The jukebox was to our left with tables and chairs scattered across the floor. Rocky and Jim were sitting at a table in the back with three other guys. Wedo and I went over to the bar and ordered a couple of beers, then sauntered to the back. Rocky looked straight into my eyes as I stood there with my beer tipped to my lips. I could see the madness, at the same instant his fist shot out and clipped the guy seated to his right. The man had been sitting with his chair cocked back. He hit the floor with a bang and Rocky was on him like a flash. Everybody was up now, wondering what to do. One punch and it was over, the guy didn't want anything to do with Rocky. He got up rubbing his jaw, looked at everyone, then went to the bar and sat down to nurse his beer. I observed Rocky getting pats on the back and everybody laughing now that it was over. Rocky was scared of getting old, I thought, and needs this type of attention to cling to his youth, what there was left of it.

I pulled Jim aside and told him about Dave being naked and marching up and down in front of his boat. "Finish your beer and we'll go have a look-see," he said.

I yelled over to Wedo and told him what we were about. We headed for the door and I stopped and yelled out, "Hey Rocky! Don't forget to get me some money. I'll be back in a half hour or so."

There was no sign of Dave anywhere. We stood by the building, peeking around the corner. Dave's boat was white, thirty-two foot long, wooden hulled, with a small cabin on it. A couple of other boats were tied forward and a couple aft. Where we stood you could only see half of the boat behind Dave's. We walked along the building, a field between us. The next building was fifty feet away. I felt exposed, creeping along the wall wondering what was wrong with this guy. All of a sudden there he was; barefoot, Levis, and a bandana around his head pirate style,

"Gotcha," Dave said. The rifle straight up and down at the ready. It must have been the lights; Dave's eyes seemed to be on fire and his mouth was formed into a menacing smile. My heart stopped right there.

"Hey ol son, it's me, Jim," he held out his hand as if Dave was a dog to see if he'd take a bite at it. "You're home now, where people love you and everything is alright," Jim said in a low quiet voice. Dave stood stock still. Jim moved slowly toward him, "It's me ol pod'ner. Jus' take it easy now, everything is gonna be fine."

I watched Jim move in on Dave, like a cowboy would move in on a nervous horse, calming him as he goes. Then Jim had a hand on the rifle and the other on the back of Dave's neck, "Easy now, son, it's alright. Nobody's going to hurt you." Jim was rubbing the back of Dave's neck talking gently as he handed the rifle back to me. I took the gun, amazed this was happening. After a while Jim got Dave turned around and walked him to the boat. They disappeared down below.

And I met this guy in jail, I thought. These fishermen were something else.

I took the gun down to the *Perfect Dawn* and set it in the cabin. I was leaning against the wall inhaling the smoke of my cigarette when Jim stepped off Dave's boat and came over toward me,

"What did you do with the rifle?" he asked.

"I put it on the Dawn, we can give it back later," I said. "What did you do with him, is he going to be alright?" I asked.

"Yeah, he'll be OK. We smoked a joint and he lay down to sleep. I should say Dave smoked the joint, I don't smoke that shit. He got shell-shocked in Korea and goes off the deep end every once in a while."

"Well, you impressed me, I didn't know whether to shit or go blind when Dave stepped out with that rifle. You're in the wrong business, man, you should be working with schizophrenics up at the state hospital," I said.

"Yeah, right; let's get the others and head over to Boys Town."

❦

I staggered out of the San Luis bar; I needed to sober up a little before Maria Lana got off work. I needed some air and food in my stomach if I was going to make it through the night. The sidewalks were vacant except for one or two stragglers a block away. I stopped in at the first café I came to and ordered a couple of chicken tacos with beans and rice. Then ordered a beer while I waited for the food and watched the old woman drop the tacos into hot grease. I thought about my trip to California and felt the urge to pick up and head out, but I wanted to see Mexico, down in the interior. I pushed the thought of California out of my head. I decided to leave right after we got back from the trip to Vera Cruz. I could hang out another month. I got my food and ate the crunchy taco, washing it down with another beer.

Out on the street I headed east and then navigated my way to the other side. The potholes were full of water, big enough to lose a truck in. A few cars were parked along the street. The Americana Club was having a slow night; a few tables were taken up by men watching the women perform their bumps and grinds. The music was loud, with three girls dancing on a small stage. Off to the right sat thirty-five lonely girls waiting to display their wares. I moved on down the side street. The night became totally dark. Street lights did not exist down this way. Darkness surrounded me and all I could see were little cubicles off to my right, with a splash of gold emanating from the lighted doorways. As I walked, a girl stuck her head out and invited me in. Sometimes two girls would invite me in. The further I walked, the darker it got, no neon lights down this way. All the light came from the rooms and small cantinas. The lights in the rooms I passed seemed soft and lonely. I looked into the rooms as I moved slowly by. A few had small children sitting up on beds or in a play pen. In several rooms women caressed each other playfully. Most of these girls were just children themselves, more prisoner than the carefree women I thought they were. It was a world without men except for the ones who come and pay for an hour or the night. It's no wonder they turned to one another for the love and affection they needed. Maria had told me of the time she married a young guy from Mississippi and moved there. It lasted three months and she came back. I asked her why and she said she couldn't stand the tight-assed American.

Walking along that dark street, I felt a hole in my gut. It could have been the alcohol, but I felt lonely all of a sudden; I wanted to see these girls laughing and having a good time, but life isn't all laughing and merriment. I felt lonely, so what, that's life. These women accepted their lot. So should I, but I didn't like it. I needed a beer.

I kept walking south on the boardwalk, afraid to step out into the street for fear of stepping into a pothole and drowning. I heard a guitar playing ahead of me then a high-pitched voice singing, "Hi-, Hi-, Hi." I followed the sound down the street and around the corner to where golden light fell out onto the boardwalk. I stopped at the door. It was a one-room building with a bar on the back wall. A group of five Mexican musicians played off to my right. A guy and gal were dancing in the middle of the floor. The man wore jeans, a white snap-down shirt and a straw cowboy hat. The woman wore a purple blouse with a multicolored skirt, pleated at the bottom. The man stood in the middle of the floor while she danced around him, throwing her skirt back and forth and stomping her heels onto the floor. Everyone seemed to be drinking tequila. Several bottles of the stuff were sitting on the bar and tables, most half full or close to empty. I could see the worm at the bottom of the bottles. These guys were out to get plowed. The idea was to drink the tequila, eat the worm, and still be standing.

I went straight for the bar hoping it was dark enough to pass for a Mexican. I knew as soon as I opened my mouth it would be over, "Da me un carta," I said, watching the dance. I got the bottle and moved along the bar to the window and took a long pull.

The dance ended a little later and everybody screamed and hollered. The bottles got tipped up and one guy started yelling. He had the worm hanging from his teeth until he bit through, and started chewing, then swallowed, and threw his arms up at the same time. These were basic farm workers who had worked hard in the field all day. They cleaned up, put on their new jeans, straw hat, and headed off to old Mexico for a night on the town. They had as much machismo ("Mexican Pride") as all Mexicans. It was a way of life for the Mexican male; as young boys they walked and talked with machismo. I knew a fight would start at some point, maybe a knife or a gun would appear, and there would be police all over the place and only one gringo. I finished the beer and got the hell out of there.

As I walked away I wondered about my own machismo, my own philosophy. Did I have any? I wasn't sure what I believed in. I knew the basics, or did I? Maybe I didn't know shit. To hell with it, Maria Lana was waiting. This would be our last night together for awhile.

CHAPTER EIGHT

A Couple of Joints

I took the last hit off the joint I'd been smoking and put it out on the floor, grinding it with the heel of my shoe. I felt stupid sitting in the little room, puffing on a marijuana cigarette. It was my second one; I had wanted to smoke a couple without any alcohol. Jim and I, with Ike this new kid who started to hang with us, stopped at a whorehouse in downtown Matamoras, Mexico. Ike, the new kid, said he had a connection downtown. We had been in Boys Town four days and were heading back to Brownsville, so why not stop and have a couple of joints. It sounded good to me. Jim said, "Fuck you guys, I don't wanta be no addict."

"Ah hell, that's an ol' wives tale," I said. "I really wanta try a couple just to see what the hell happens. You can wait in the car."

We had pulled up in front of a big, old, yellow house in the middle of the block. A few cars were parked along the street with several brightly colored houses on both sides of the street. A few people were walking along the sidewalk. Ike and I walked up the steps onto the porch and through the doorway, entering a dark hall. Ike told the guy what I wanted, and then disappeared off to the side someplace. I followed the Mexican down a dark hall way with doors on both sides. The Mexican stopped at the third door.

"You wait," he said.

I stepped into the room. A bare light bulb hung from the ceiling, shades were pulled over the windows, paint peeling off the walls. I sat down on a dirty old bed, the blankets were rolled up in a bunch, stains on the mattress. My heart was beating so hard I couldn't sit still. I stood up ready to leave when a girl brought in two rolled cigarettes.

I smoked both joints down to the nub. Now I felt stupid sitting there. "This was a bunch of bullshit, the two joints were nothing," I said to myself, getting up from the bed. I felt a little dizzy, that was all. I should never have trusted that little weasel Ike. Ike had a small rodent looking face, his eyes close together, a three week growth of peach fuzz, and dark, greasy hair combed straight back. He wore a pair of slacks that were new in the nineteen-forties, and old, scuffed up brown shoes.

I opened the door and stepped out into the hall which was darker than I remembered. It seemed a long way to the front door, as I moved through the hall and out the door, I had the feeling that somebody might try to stop me. I stood on the front porch looking up and down the street, feeling something was different, but couldn't put my finger on it. Small groups of Mexicans stood along the sidewalk. My cheek had acquired a quiver somehow.

I was watching the closest group, of Mexicans when one of the men gave me a menacing look. I stepped back a little, fear rising into my chest. I looked down at the green Chevy, Jim sat behind the wheel, straight as a board, head tilted a little forward as if he were staring down at a cobra. This time the fear grabbed me like an ice-cold hand in my gut. They've killed him! I thought. I ran down the five steps of the porch and over to the car grabbing Jim. He jumped a half a foot and let out a holler you could hear for a mile. The fear left me momentarily, I was so startled. "You're alive!" I said, dumbfounded.

"Hell yes I'm alive you dumb-ass, get in the fucking car."

I thought I detected a sense of urgency in his voice. I ran around and jumped in the other side, "Let's get the hell outta here while we still can!" I yelled, the fear was back hard and strong.

"Just hang on to your horse's pod'ner, We still have ta wait fer Ike."

"Ike, I forgot about him. He's not outta there yet?"

"Nope, he'll be along." Jim laid his head back on the seat, and pulled the cap down over his eyes.

I looked through the front windshield. The sidewalks were starting to fill with people. All of a sudden it hit me; these people were going to kill us! We have to get out of here now! I turned to Jim. A Mexican stuck his head down by the window, "You wait for friend?"

Jim nodded affirmative.

The Mexican didn't speak very good English. He rattled off a bunch of Spanish, and all I could get was "lick" and "blood."

The son of a bitch killed one of the girls! I visualized the girl lying in a pool of blood, Ike bent over her licking the blood off his finger. I shuddered at the thought. That's what all these people are about! "They're going to kill us!" I yelled, rocking back and forth in my seat.

The sidewalks were full now. Five older kids were sitting on the hood of our car. My side window was open an inch or two; when a ten-year-old kid grabbed the top and put his face against the glass, bending his nose and sticking his tongue out. A police car pulled up a half block ahead of us. I strained my neck to see what was happening. I looked in the side rear view mirror, another cop car pulled in a half block behind us. I sat there squirming, trying to figure this out. I was petrified. A military truck came by and made a right turn a hundred feet ahead of us and disappeared around the corner. In my mind's eye I could see the military truck stop and six soldiers get out and unload a cannon from the back, turn it toward the street and start to load it with four-inch shells two feet long. I was totally engulfed in horror, holding onto the dash, rocking back and forth, screaming, "We gotta get outta here, damn it, we gotta get outta here!"

In the distance I heard Jim say, "I told ya not to be smokin' that shit, this'll learn ya."

The back door opened and Ike jumped in, "Man! That was the greatest, best pussy I had all week. We can head back to the States now, I'm ready." He looked over at me, "What's the matter with you?"

"Let's get the hell outta here!" I yelled.

He looked at Jim, "Well?"

"Shit man, you oughta know, you took him in there to smoke that stuff." Jim started the car and slowly pulled away from the curb.

"Can't you go any faster? We gotta get outta here," I yelled, still rocking back and forth, my fear ebbing as we started to move through the crowd.

"Hey man! You got a little paranoid there huh, like, man, don't sweat it, it happens to the best of us. It'll be over in a little bit," Ike said.

"There's over a hundred Mexicans here. What's the deal anyway, Ike?" Jim asked, putting a cigarette between his lips, eyes on the road.

"Hell, I don't know; Some Saints day. It's like, man, a big celebration." Ike leaned up and laid his arms on the back of Jim's seat, "The parade's about to start anytime now," he said.

"Parade?" I said. Knowing didn't help much, the fear was still there. I kept my eyes closed for a time, it seemed to help. Then I spotted the bridge. It was as if a big boulder had been released from my chest. Now all I had was a hole the size of Grand Canyon.

The Border Patrol passed us through with no problem. A couple hundred feet farther I told Jim to stop. I got out of the car and got down on my knees and kissed the ground. I was feeling great again. I couldn't believe the fear went away that fast. I got back into the car and said, "Getting high in a small dark room by yourself, and in a foreign country, isn't too smart. I'll never do that shit again… let's go get us a beer," I said.

CHAPTER NINE

The Storm

The time had arrived. Vera Cruz, here we come!

It was the tenth of January and fishing had fallen off. Rocky had decided to leave earlier than expected, and that was all right with me. The boat was loaded and ready to go. The bins were full to the ceilings with ice. We had enough food to last a month, the meat would last two or three weeks, then it would be whatever we could catch or trade for, probably a lot of fish. We had been ready for three days waiting for a weather window. We needed at least three days of clear weather to get started. It was an overcast day, with a hint of blue in the sky, which gave me hope for a nice day. Wedo came into the pilot house where I was sitting in the captain's chair and said, "Let's get all the lines aboard except the bow and stern lines. I just talked to Rocky on the phone and he's on his way over now. So we're finally going to get under way. I'm going to start the engines. Make sure you disconnect that water hose."

An hour later I looked over to the east and said goodbye to Padre Island. We were sailing into open water. I was at the wheel heading in a southwesterly direction. The waves came from behind the boat, pushing us right along. I looked down into the cabin and saw Rocky unfold a big chart and lay it out on the table. I could tell he was a little nervous working out a course I could steer by. It isn't everyday you shoot across the Gulf of Mexico. Twenty minutes later he yelled up the numbers, and I brought the boat over on course. We'd be on this course for the next five days. The weather was clearing nicely. Jim on the Linda Lu was a quarter mile off our stern rolling gracefully from side to side. It seemed prudent to sail with another boat in case problems might arise, like getting holed, or the engine quitting, or a multitude of other things that go wrong on a fishing boats. The days passed quickly as we cruised south. By the third day the weather started to warm up. Rocky, Wedo and I each did four-hour watches with eight hours off. I did a lot of reading while off watch and drank too much coffee. I'd sit out on deck in the sunshine and roll with movement of the boat, not a care in world. My body turned to a dark brown and I looked like a native.

I was sitting up on the foredeck outside the cabin reading when I heard Wedo yell, "Land ho, Skipper!" I stood up on my knees, with my elbows on the side-rail, and looked out over the water. Through the haze I could see land. It was a little after noon of our fifth day out. We kept on course for an hour and a half and then turned to run parallel to the land, still heading in a southerly direction. I stepped up into the pilot house as Rocky said, "We'll drop the nets at Rock of Botia. It will take about two or three hours to get there, so give me a call when you see the rock." He went down and crawled into his bunk.

"What the hell is Rock of Botia?" I asked.

"It's a great big rock with bird shit all over it. You'll see when we get there. I mean there is a ton of bird shit on this rock," Wedo said, jumping back into the captain's chair and reaching for a smoke. "It's a landmark. The area around it is all mountains and jungle."

"Where is Vera Cruz from here?" I asked, "Let me have one those smokes will ya."

"It's back to the north of us, and I hope the gun boats are all nicely tied up at their docks, but you know they're not. I suppose they will be out sniffing the waters looking for fishing boats inside the continental limits," Wedo said, flipping the cigarette at me.

I caught the smoke with my left hand and lit it. "What's that got to do with us? We'll be fishing more then three miles off shore."

"Mexico has made their continental line eleven miles off shore and that means we are supposed to stay offshore eleven miles. It's a bunch of shit, but the United States gave the Mexican government three old boats for their east coast and two for the west coast. Now they hunt for us every fuck`in night and think nothing about shooting over our bow. If we take off they start shooting at us for real and there's no way we're not going to take off," Wedo said as he blew a smoke ring toward the ceiling.

"Man you can't blow smoke rings for shit. Watch this," I said, blowing two rings, one smaller than the other, the smaller one going through the big one. "Now that's perfection my man. I had a lot of practice sitting in jail.

What happens if we heave too, and let them board?" I asked.

"They confiscate all our gear. The nets, cables, everything then try to ransom the boat back to the company that owns it," Wedo said.

"You're right, that does sound like a bunch of shit." I stood in the doorway watching the land get closer. "If you want anything give me a holler. I'll be out on deck."

The sun was on its way down and we were coasting in close to shore. The rock, still a half mile away, stood a hundred feet in the air. It looked like it was half covered with snow and sat in a little cove with a mountainous background. The mountains seemed to go up forever. The land was all jungle, a blend of greens and black. At the waters edge the mountain continued its descent and the water got deep fast.

When we dropped the anchor we were in real close to the shore and it seemed as though we were sitting on the side of the mountain. The sun had passed over the top of the mountain and we were in deep shade. Not yet dark, the jungle was an awesome sight. I felt like the boat was an insignificant speck against the backdrop of this mountainous jungle. I sat wondering what it was like in amongst all those trees; and then I saw a little boat moving toward us.

When Wedo started cooking dinner, I went out on the back deck and started straightening out the nets, getting the gear ready to fish. We would drop the nets tonight. Twenty minutes latter I felt a bump alongside the boat. I walked over to the rail and looked down. A Mexican stared up at me with a big smile on his face. A young boy of ten or eleven sat in the front of the boat and a four-foot stalk of green bananas lay between them. The Mexican took the straw hat off his head and rattled off a bunch of Spanish at me.

"Kay pa-so, amigo, un momento," I said cupping a hand around my mouth, "Hey Rocky we got company, you better come talk to this guy, I can't understand what he's saying," I yelled out over the deck.

Rocky came around the corner of the cabin with a cigarette hanging from his lips, and put his foot up on the rail then started talking in Spanish to the Mexican. I went back to work. A few minutes later Rocky had a stalk of bananas in his arms. He laid them down on the hatch cover and pulled out his knife, cutting the stalk in two.

"What are we going to do with a bunch of green bananas?" I asked, walking over to the hatch.

"Pick up that bunch there and take them down to the engine room. Tie them out of the way and check them about nine this evening. They should be ripe by then."

"I don't believe that shit," I said. reaching down for a stalk of bananas.

"O ye of little faith, pay attention," Rocky said.

Sure enough, I went back at nine o'clock and big yellow bananas were hanging there. They were some of the best bananas I've ever eaten. I decided to pick out a couple of large fish for our Mexican friend.

We fished right off the rock for the next eight nights; running with no lights except the red and green running lights. When it was time to pick up the nets we would turn on the big lights on the back deck just long enough to get the nets aboard and back in the water. Then we'd turn on a small light to head out the shrimp and dump the trash. Everything was going along fine. I was standing outside the cabin with my foot up on the rail, drinking a cup coffee and smoking a cigarette. All of a sudden there was a big flash of light offshore. "Hey Rocky, did you see that light?" I yelled, running up into the cabin.

Rocky was hanging up the speaker on the VHF as I came through the door. "Start getting those nets up, Pronto! The gunboat is just offshore a couple of miles and moving in quick," he said, jumping out of his chair and grabbing the throttle to speed up the boat. Wedo ran out the side door. I turned around heading the way I came in, hitting the light switch as I went, grabbing the foul weather gear hanging by the door. Wedo had the wench running and the cables coming in at a faster pace then usual. I threw his gear down on the hatch. "Your gear is lying behind you," I yelled, getting in position to grab the lazy line when the bag came up. It seemed to take forever, but it finally broke the surface and I latched onto the line. There was a three to four foot chop on the water and as soon as the nets hit the deck our lights went out. It took a couple of minutes for my eyes to adjust to the darkness. Rocky was already running full bore and we were going through the chop rockin' and a rollin'. The nets had two to three hundred pounds of fish in each one and they were sliding all over the deck. It was a lot like trying to harness a couple of huge boa constrictors, you just can't get your hands around them.

As I was trying to tame these two nets, shots rang out, close by. I stood up and looked around. Everything was pitch black, then a little light came on. It was an emergency light under the overhang of the cabin. Wedo came over and we both manhandled the nets one at a time over to the rail and got them tied down. Shots rang out again, this time it was like a machine gun, rat-a-tat-tat. The wind was blowing, the engine screaming and water hitting me full in the face. Five boats had been fishing this area but we scattered as if the devil himself was hot on our trail. Every once in awhile we'd see a flash of light, a little gunfire, but that was it. I think the Mexican Navy just wanted to keep us on our toes. They couldn't just let us fish in their waters. After a while we'd think it was our right.

The *Perfect Dawn* moved in shore and headed in a northerly direction. When we thought it safe, we moved offshore and kept heading north, up past Vera Cruz. Daylight found us heading out the shrimp under a warm sun. We had to get the fish iced down quickly.

The next couple of weeks went along nicely; no gunboats. I read my books and laid around in the sun while Rocky and Wedo slept. Every once in a while I would dive off the bow of the boat to swim, but barracuda would jump into my mind as I hit the water. With no one else around, swimming wasn't much fun. Then came the storm.

℘

I sat up feeling drugged. My tongue stuck to the top of my mouth, the boat was rocking gently. I needed some coffee to keep my eyes open. It was five in the evening. We would drop the nets in a couple of hours. I pulled on my rubber boots, stood up, threw the sleeping bag up over the bunk, and went up the ladder to the galley to get the coffee going.

I'd stayed up later then usual this morning. After the work was done, around ten, I sat out on deck in the warm sun reading till noon. I was paying for it now. The heat of the day was still with us. I looked out over the ocean. It was smooth as glass with big swells rolling under us. The anchor was holding well, not dragging. The sky was brilliant as the sun headed for the west. All was quiet except for the creaking of the boat, hanging cups gently hitting bulkheads. Wedo was out on the back deck making sure everything was ready to go when we'd drop the nets in a couple of hours. Rocky was up forward in the pilothouse talking on the VHF. I heard "Gawd have mercy." I wondered as I lit the flame on the butane stove if he could ever talk on the radio without using that phrase.

The next instant Rocky was in the doorway yelling, "Get everything tied down! The winds are blowing a hundred, two hours away!" I could tell by his face he wasn't kidding. I bolted the coffee pot down as the engines started up. Rocky already had the anchor coming up as I went out the door to let Wedo know what was happening. I ran forward to secure the anchor.

I looked across the water at the *Linda Lu;* they were hustling to get their anchor up, as we were. Five of us were anchored offshore, several hundred miles from home. A hundred-mile-an-hour wind is no place for a small fishing boat. There was only one place to go, Pie Island off Vera Cruz. It would take at least two hours to get there. Rocky had the engines at full throttle. We were moving as fast as we could without blowing the engines. Jim on the Linda Lu had gotten ahead of us. We were right on his tail. The other three boats were falling in behind us. It was still a beautiful afternoon.

The *Linda Lu* and the *Perfect Dawn* were both steel-hulled boats, seventy feet in length. The other three boats were wooden, and the last boat in line was only thirty-two feet.

Wedo and I got everything lashed down on the decks, then went forward to check the cabin. "I think we got it all tied down pretty good," I said, coming through the door.

"Pat, come take this wheel, Wedo, you come with me, we gotta get that engine room squared away," Rocky said. They ran out the side door and headed for the back deck.

It had taken us fifteen minutes to get underway, another thirty to get the back deck secured, and already the day had changed. The seas were building, small whitecaps covered the ocean, big, dark clouds were on the march from the north. The *Linda Lu's* nose was plowing through the water; her propeller was up and out of the water. The autopilot was working fine on the *Perfect Dawn;* I just let her do the work staying with the *Linda Lu* which was off to our right several hundred feet. The other three boats were spread out behind us. The race was on for Pie Island.

Minutes were clicking away, and the seas got bigger. Huge rollers came up from behind, pushing the boat from side to side and foreword. Massive clouds collected overhead, darkness was setting in. A big wave came over the back. The whole deck was awash with rushing water. I took hold of the wheel and got us back on track, the autopilot was out of commission. I tried to spot the *Linda Lu,* the wind was blowing water everywhere. Every once in a while I'd see her, then the waves would engulf her. I couldn't tell how hard the wind was blowing, but it sounded like a freight train going through the rigging. I was singing at the top of my voice and jumping in the air; it was like riding a bucking bronco. Rocky came through the door and took one look at me, "What the fuck you doing, you got that reef in sight yet?"

"Not yet. How in hell am I supposed to see it, with all this water all over the goddamm place. I just seen the *Linda Lu's* ass-end over there," I pointed off to our right, "Then it just disappeared underwater."

"Let's have that fucking wheel before you kill us all." Rocky took hold of the wheel with one hand and wiped the windows with the other. He peered out. After a minute he stepped back and said, " The reef is dead ahead."

I stepped to the window cupping my hands to keep out the light and looked out. For the life of me I couldn't see a thing except a mountain of water. All of a sudden a form took shape behind the phosphorous and the water, it all seemed to blend together. "I see it!" I yelled, stepping back on Wedo's foot. I looked up to see his face; he didn't look so good holding on to the door frame. His long blond hair soaked tight around his neck; wet mustache hanging down around his mouth, his eyes staring straight ahead into the darkness. I put my arm around his shoulder. "Man, this is great fun. You ever see water this high? You might never get to see anything as wild as this again. You got to enjoy it while you can, my man."

"There's the hole. Jim's just going through," Rocky said.

I looked back through the windows again; all I could see were angry waves smashing up against the reef. The spotlight on the roof set off the phosphorous, it was all aglow, and we were still a couple of hundred yards away. The *Linda Lu* had disappeared behind a wall of waves. "If it will just hold off a few more minutes, we'll be through," Rocky said in a low voice, as if praying.

But that wasn't to be, as all hell broke loose. I thought the wind had been blowing hard, but now it was deafening. Darkness was coming on fast and the hole disappeared. Monstrous waves broke on the reef and we were heading right for it.

"You mother-fucking bastard, why didn't ya wait?" Rocky yelled, turning the wheel all the way over to port trying to bring the boat around into the wind.

For a shaky minute there I thought we were going right up on that reef, but then the prop took hold and started clawing its way out of there. Waves were coming over the bow and cabin non-stop. One minute we'd be under water and the next we'd be on top a wave. Then the wave would disappear and we'd drop down thirty feet or so with a tooth-rattling suddenness. The soles of our feet would leave the deck and we'd be in mid-air coming down with a crash, only to be engulfed in water again. I don't know how far off that reef we got, but Rocky was trying to get to open water. We had to head out to sea, and into the storm.

I was holding onto the ledge under the windows with both hands. The bronco ride was over; now it felt like being on an elevator as it drops a couple of floors. The thought never occurred to me that we might die right there, I was having a ball. I'd yell on the way down and come up laughing.

"What the hell you think this is, some kind of picnic?" Rocky yelled at me, "Knock that shit off! I can't think with you yelling all over the fucking place!"

We had been pushing into the storm for a half hour. Rocky's face was stern, his hat squared on his head. I tried to grasp the gravity of the situation, I couldn't, I was having too much fun.

"Wedo, this is going to be a battle, so head on down and get some sleep. You might have to take over the wheel in a couple of hours," Rocky said.

"Who in hell can sleep in this shit," Wedo said, but he went out through the door and down to his bunk.

I had realized Rocky was scared, by his anger. People demonstrate fear in different ways; Rocky's was anger. I didn't say anything. When I was in the Navy I'd been in a couple of storms like this off Cape Hatteras, so this wasn't my first big storm. If you trust your boat, then you can have fun.

I looked out the windows and all around the boat for lights, but there were none. "Well, I don't see a boat any place, so maybe I'll go fill that thermos with some hot coffee," I said. I had quieted down now and went into the galley to get the coffee. Pouring coffee into a thermos in that weather was like standing on a board that was balanced on a rock, when some asshole pulls out the rock. Damn near impossible, but with great delicacy I was able to get it done.

Rocky was fighting the wheel and cussing when I fell through the door. "Just jam the sucker into the seat, I don't have time for it now," Rocky yelled. I jammed the thermos between the two cushions in the captain's chair.

"Here take this wheel a second, I gotta piss."

I stepped over to the wheel and took hold,

"Ya got it?" he asked.

"Yeah I got it," I said. When he let go, the wheel almost threw me against the wall, but I stuck my foot into the wall and pushed with everything I had. By the time I had some control over it Rocky was back.

"OK. I got it," he said. I moved over to the side and let him have it gladly.

℘

We'd been at this for a couple of hours, and my head started pounding. I was getting one of the worst headaches I'd ever had. The fun and games were over. The wind had reached its maximum force and seemed to be slackening a little, but it was still a force to be reckoned with. "I have to lie down man, my head is killing me. I'll wake Wedo," I said, walking out the door and down to my bunk. "Wedo, Wake up and go stay with Rocky till this wind slacks up. I gotta lie down, my head is splitting."

"I'm awake," he said.

I was asleep before my head hit the pillow.

✑

The storm lasted till four in the morning, then was gone as quick as it came. I came alive around six, everything was calm. I lay there listening for the banging of the waves, but nothing. We were still moving through the water, the engines purring along. When I stood up I could see that Rocky was asleep in his bunk. I stepped up into the galley. The coffee pot was hot, I unbolted it, and poured a cup, "Hey Wedo, you want a cop of coffee?"

"Sure," he said.

I went into the pilot house. We were heading in a southerly direction. The coast of Mexico was off our starboard beam, (right side), a sandy beach stretched out for miles. It looked uninhabited. "Where we heading?" I asked.

"We're going to take a few days off. Pie Island is the next stop. They got some pretty little women there and I'm gonna get me one," he sang.

"What in hell happened last night? Why didn't you wake me?"

"It wasn't necessary, I thought you needed the sleep. Anyway it was Rocky's idea. We lost three boats last night, I think. So far that's all I heard about."

"Well what happened to the men on those boats. Did they all drown or what?"

"They're missing right now. The Mexican Coast Guard could of picked them up. I was talking to Jim on the *Linda Lu* a while ago. He's trying to find out. He said he'd let me know when he found anything out."

"Ain't that a bitch. Maybe we should move inshore incase we can see anything," I said.

"Calling the *Perfect Dawn,* this is the *Linda Lu,* over." A voice came over the VHF.

Wedo picked up the mike, "This is the *Perfect Dawn.* What's happen'in

Cap'n?" he said.

"Well, I got a little news. The Mexicans picked everybody up. Bill and Jerry on the *Miss Law* went right up on the reef. That little 32-footer just sat there high and dry; those two assholes jumped off onto the reef, cut up they're legs pretty bad, they're in the hospital, The *Venture* went up on the beach north of here. And the *Storm Rider* was taking on water when the Mexicans came up to save the day. Of course they lost all their fish and rigging. The Mexicans will take that. And ransom the boat back to the company they work for. Over."

"Lord have mercy, Cap'n," Wedo said, trying to sound like Rocky "Well, I'm glad everybody made it. That was sure one hell of a blow. I'm moving inshore now, maybe we'll see something. We should be rounding the island in about two hours."

The sky was a crystal blue and the Gulf waters were flat, no wind. The sun was getting warm, so I took off my shirt. We got into forty fathoms and started running along the beach. It felt like we were right on the beach. The water starts getting deep quick off the Mexican coast. There was empty beach as far as the eye could see. After twenty minutes of running, I thought I could see a boat on the beach. I went and got the binoculars to get a closer look and sure enough, there sat the *Venture* lying high up on the beach. All we could do was look at it. That boat was going to be there a while.

We eased offshore and kept running until we saw the reef. With the reef on our port side we made for the Island. We passed the *Miss Law* sitting up on the reef, pretty as a picture, "She'll still be there in ten years, you watch and see," Wedo said.

"It sure makes a guy feel good to have a steel hull under him. After all the bashing we took last night, we didn't even lose a cup," I said.

I took a cigarette out of my hip pocket and stepped out on deck watching for the break in the reef.

"Give Rocky a call, will ya?" Wedo said.

CHAPTER TEN

Vera Cruz

The reef was a natural breakwater; once through the scene changed. Vera Cruz could be seen off to the right. A seawall ran along the beach to a dock that branched out at right angles. Two ships were tied to the dock; one a merchant and the other an English navy ship. Large warehouses filled the background north of the dock. The dock was busy with longshoremen running forklifts, moving boxes here and there. A few Mexican fishing boats were unloading their fish. Behind the seawall there were shops, restaurants, and bars. A hillside full of multicolored houses rounded off the panorama; the colors were wonderful reds, pinks, blues, and yellows splashed over the hill. Twenty or so small boats were on the move, some heading toward the other fishing boats, some heading toward shore. All moving their own contraband, women, booze, and dope or whatever else a man might want. Two boats were heading our way.

Several American fishing boats were anchored off the island. Wedo bore off to his left and headed in that direction. I heard Rocky moving in the cabin, then he stepped up into the pilothouse; his hat on the back of his head, a cigarette between his lips. "A much better entrance than last night" he said, lighting his cigarette, "Call Jim up on the radio."

I looked back at the town. Fernando Cortes had landed in this bay in 1519 with some 550 Spaniards. He then burned all eleven ships and marched to Mexico City. Montezuma did little to stop him and he vanquished a whole people. There's a lot of history here, I thought, then my mind went back to the bum boats.

The two small boats I'd spotted earlier were now alongside us, cruising at the same speed. Both boats had three women and two men in them. They were smiling and waving. I waved back feeling good, knowing it was time to party. "Hey, Rocky, look at this!" I yelled.

Rocky stepped out the door and waved, yelling something in Spanish. The two boats veered off, gunning their engines. "What'd you say to 'em?" I asked.

"I told them to come back when we were anchored and bring two bottles of whiskey with them."

Wedo stepped out the door and yelled "Hey, Rocky, Jim's on the radio and wants us to raft up beside him. You wanta talk to him?"

Rocky turned and went into the cabin. I went forward to flake out the bow line. I got the spring line and stern line ready to go if we were going to be rafting up. Twenty minutes later we were tied up next to the Linda Lu, which was tied next to the Miss Pearl. Cap'n Art on the Pearl had some things stolen the night before while he and the rig man were ashore. He thought it might deter the Mexicans if we rafted up together. We all thought it was a good idea.

"Hell of a blow, sure glad you people made it," Jim said. He was sitting on the back hatch cover all laid back, holding a bottle of tequila. "Yes sir, I drove right on in here and dropped the hook and it got downright pleasant."

"Bullshit," Rocky said. "That sucker was blowing a hundred if it was blowing a minute. You forget I was right behind your ass." Rocky sat down next to Jim and took the offered bottle. Art stepped over from the Pearl and joined them.

"I hear you lost a few things last night," Rocky said.

"A few things, hell; those bastards stole my generator. That thing weighs a couple hundred pounds. How in hell you think they got it off the boat?" Art asked.

"How in hell do I know, those crafty devils get more inventive every year." Rocky said. "Hey Wedo! Come on over and get a drink if you want."

Wedo and I were hanging the nets to dry. I tied off the line I was holding and went over. Art pulled out three rolled joints. "Man, this in some wicked shit, you're not even going to believe it," he said, lighting the first one. I took a drink out of the bottle and waited for the joint to come around, remembering my last episode with this stuff. Oh well, what the hell.

A half hour later I stood up and it felt like someone had increased the gravity, and time slowed way down. I started heading for the *Perfect Dawn*, it felt like it took a long time to get from one boat to the next. All of a sudden

I was on the other boat, I looked down to find a third of a bottle of tequila in my hand. I wondered how long I had been standing there and where was I going. I looked back and I could see the guys talking back and forth, then the whole thing hit me, the cosmic truth, and I started laughing. I laughed so hard tears rolled down my cheeks. I got to the cabin and through the door, the laughter just kept coming. I tried to remember what I was laughing about, but could not and that became hilarious. I got a piece of bread and put some peanut butter on it, and went down to my bunk to collect my thoughts.

Rocky walked in and looked down at me, "What the hell is wrong with you?" he asked.

I looked up at him, I couldn't stop laughing. Then the lights went out and I fell back onto the bunk.

Something kept flapping me in the face. This big black bird was pulling on me. I soared out of unconsciousness at the speed of light, and my eyes jumped open. It was like coming out of a black hole so fast my brain couldn't keep up. I was sitting on my bunk with this euphoric feeling, wondering where the bird was. I shook my head to clear it, but I couldn't bring it down to reality. I didn't know if I liked this feeling or not. I saw the bottle of tequila sitting on the floor and reached for it. Even a good stiff drink of that stuff didn't help. I lifted myself up off the bunk and realized how light I felt. Outside the cabin in the fresh air life didn't seem bad at all.

I could hear the water splashing up against the boat, the rigging creaking in the wind, but no sound other than that. Nobody was on board. I looked around the boat but saw nothing. I took the bottle to the back deck, sat on the hatch cover and lit a cigarette wondering where everybody went. There didn't seem to be anybody on Jim's boat either. I was sitting there trying to think what to do when I looked up. I jumped half a foot, "Jesus Christ! You scared the shit out of me. Who the hell are you?"

A man on Jim's boat stood looking down at me. He was well over six foot, huge, long, black hair down to his shoulders and a long beard hanging off his face. He wore no shirt or shoes, a pair of Levis is all he had on. Samson came to mind as I looked up at him.

"I'm Ben, rig man on the Pearl. Everyone went on into town. They jumped into a bum boat and off they went. They said I was to tell you to hang with the boat till they got back."

"Hang with the boat, what kind of shit is that? I wanted to go into town, too." I lifted the bottle and took a good, long pull, "Damn! That pisses me off." I looked at the bottle. "You got anything besides this shit? It tastes like kerosene."

"Ya, the Mexicans just brought out three cases of Corona. It's a Mexican beer and tastes pretty good, too." He turned and went over to the Pearl, and was back in less than two minutes with six beers. He jumped over onto the *Perfect Dawn*, sat down on the hatch cover. Set the beers down and pulled a bag out of his hip pocket and started rolling a joint.

"What the hell is that stuff anyway? It almost knocked my head off."

"This is gold, man. The Indians take this stuff to go on a spiritual journey. After three days of smoking, a vision appears and tells them how to live the spiritual life."

"I don't know if I want anymore of that shit or not," I said, thinking back on that bird flapping in my face when I woke.

Ben stuck the joint between his lips and lit it, then took a drag and inhaled deeply. "I was hanging out down in the Keys when I met this hip guy that just got back from Mexico. He had been living with the Indians down in Yucatan." Ben let the smoke out slowly, "What a rush! Man, he told me about this stuff. I've been trying to get here for a year. I'm on my way down to the Yucatan now. Live with the Indians and maybe learn some of their secrets. You never know, I might find enlightenment." He handed me the joint. I took a short hit this time, telling myself to pay attention. I also drank a half bottle of beer trying to counteract the pot. "I thought you had to attain enlightenment, like meditate. Hey man, where you from anyway?" I asked.

"The boat's from Tampa. Me, I'm from New York. Lived in the Village for a couple of years; met some great people there, all kinds of people. In the Village you can get started on the road to enlightenment, but you can't lose your inhibitions, got to go to the source. I will find a shaman and become his student. This is my destiny, to live with the Indians. I came down to Florida and started working the shrimp boats hoping to get one over to Yucatan. But this is as close as I could get."

We sat there silent for a while smoking the joint and drinking the beer. I thought about the bird, and tried to picture an Indian medicine man. Maybe this was my destiny too, to go live with the Indians in Yucatan.

"I gotta quit smoking this shit," I said. "I want to go party in Vera Cruz, that's what I want to do." I got up and started pacing, trying to clear my head. "I don't wanta live with no goddamn Indians and be sitting around smoking this shit; I won't have a brain left after a month. What are you going to do, just jump off the boat and take off for the Yucatan?" I asked.

116

"Yeah man, that's what I'm going to do." Ben said. "I told the Mexican in the bum boat to come back in a couple hours, and I'd have my stuff ready. I was over in town yesterday and met this beautiful chick who comes from the Yucatan. She just loves hell out of me. She wants to go with me. We'll leave in a day or two."

"You're serious," I said, taking a big hit on the joint. "What about the job man? You can't just jump ship. What's Art going to do about a rig man?" I reached down for the bottle of tequila and took a drink. I was feeling no pain by this time and thinking that making off for the Yucatan didn't sound like a bad idea. I was getting sick of this job anyway. Hell, didn't they just leave me here and go into town to get laid and have a good time.

"There are four guys on the beach right now who need a job. Their boats got lost yesterday. Have you forgotten? What the hell, Art will work it out one way or the other." Ben stood up and started back toward his boat, "I'm going to get my stuff; if you wanta go, get your shit together."

I sat there thinking and took another drink of the tequila. What the hell, I thought, and staggered off to get my stuff.

స్౭

The bum boat lurched away from the *Perfect Dawn*. I was sitting on the gunnels looking at Vera Cruz as the boat picked up speed and over the side I went. I was holding onto the sides while the Mexican slowed down. He thought it was pretty funny. I'm not sure how he felt the next three times, but the cold water sobered me up a little. We banged into a piling on arriving at the pier I was able to stay in the boat this time. A steel ladder ran straight up to the top of the pier with ten rungs to climb, so up we went. It was about one o' clock in the afternoon. I looked back at the English ship. The sailor's were moving smartly back and forth on deck. I was glad it was them and not me. Ben and I headed toward town where the action was.

స్౭

At the end of the pier was a string of two-story white buildings with a boardwalk in front. The bottom floors were all glass. The top floors were apartments and offices. Once leaving the pier the road continued west, heading up hill. At the corner Ben and I turned into a bar on the first floor of one of the white buildings. It had a big spacious room with two doors on the front, one on the street side where we came from, and one more at the far end leading into the next building. The bar was on the west side of the room with twenty small tables taking up the south side of the room.

Ben and I sat at the bar, ordered a couple of beers and looked around the room, lo and behold, there sat Wedo in the back with a couple of other fishermen and three girls. He hadn't seen me enter. I sat drinking my beer trying to come up with a good reason why I wasn't on the boat, it was quite sobering. I picked up my pack and told Ben I was going to change into some dry clothes, and headed for the restroom. Wedo looked up just as my feet hit the floor, I moved quickly into the restroom, but not quick enough.

Wedo was in the doorway before I could get my shirt off. The room was six-by-six with two commodes and a table against the back wall. One lonely light bulb hung high up on the ceiling. No windows and only the one door, nowhere to run. "What the fuck you doing here? You're supposed to be on the boat. Man, is Rocky going to be pissed!" Wedo stood there glaring at me

"Don't fuck with me right now," I said with as much anger as I could muster up. "I was loaded on that shit everybody was smoking, and the tequila didn't help either. It seemed like a good idea at the time. Hell, I fell out of that bum boat five times. I'm just now getting sober enough to figure out what happened," I threw the wet shirt on the table, picked up my bag, I started rummaging through it, looking for a shirt of some kind. Wedo started laughing behind me. I turned looking over my shoulder,

"Well, you're here now. We might as well have a beer. Come on out when you're finished," he said, turning toward the bar. As I watched him leave I hoped Rocky would be as easy.

I heard a table or chair crashing as I came out the door. A woman was yelling in Mexican. Two men were down on the floor wrestling. I walked over to the bar and picked up my beer, the better to watch the fight. I realized one of guys was Wedo. This should be really good, I sat back to enjoy the fight. Ben leaned over and said "There was a couple of guys in here yesterday that got into a battle and nobody could stop them before the police got here. When the cops arrived they didn't say jack shit to anybody, they just walked up and shot both men. Didn't kill them, but didn't do them any good either. The bartender says police will be here in a couple minutes, so if you want your partner to be healthy tomorrow you should probably break this thing up." I looked at Ben to see if he was pulling my leg, he looked me straight in the eye and gave me a shit-eatin' grin. "Your call," he said, tipping up his glass.

I moved quickly off the stool and into the fray. I didn't think either one could have fought their way out of a paper bag. Wedo was in the process of throwing a punch when I grabbed his arm and put my hand out to hold the other guy back long enough to yell at Wedo. "The police are on their way! It's time to quit or we'll all land in jail." The other fisherman grabbed my forearm with both hands, pulled me past him, and headed for Wedo. I got a hold of his shirt collar and yanked him back yelling, "The cops are coming, Goddamn it, and you don't have any papers to be down here in Mexico, so you'd better cool it, man, or we'll all be in jail."

The fisherman stopped and looked at me through bleary eyes as if seeing me for the first time.

"Do you hear me? The cops are on their way."

A couple of seconds later everybody rushed for a seat. The bartender got the table upright. I sat down on the stool next to Ben and lit a cigarette. A minute later two brown-clad policemen walked in casually looked around. Big guns on their hips, and long black billy clubs hung from their wrists. They walked over to the bar and talked to the bartender quietly for a minute, then walked out just as casually as they had come in.

Wedo walked up behind us and put his arms around Ben's and my shoulders, with his head in close to my ear he said, "Everything cool man." His heavy breathing made my neck itch and I shoved his arm off my back,

"The bartender said they came in yesterday and just shot two guys, boom, boom, no problem. You're a lucky mother, asshole," I said, standing up and putting a foot on the stool, I was feeling no pain and felt like if he kept leaning on me I'd fall over.

"Hey' amigo! Dos tequilas for my friends here," Wedo said. "I love ya, man." He tried to give me a hug. I wasn't feeling huggable. I picked up the shot of tequila and downed it in one gulp. I stuck a piece of lemon between my teeth, sucking in the juice then licking a little salt off the inside of my thumb, shaking my head all the while. It burned all the way down. Then Ben said, "Bartender, tres mas tequila, por favor," and once again tip the glass, bite the lemon, lick the salt. I looked at the other two through hazy eyes, and said, "What the hell. Bartender, tres mas tequila, por favor and again tip the glass, bite the lemon, lick the salt, but this time I was in trouble I had to sit down before I fell down. The world started to revolve around me. I grabbed onto the bar and held on for dear life. It was a hell of a ride. Nobody else was aware of my spinning predicament. After a minute the world started slowing down, came to a stop, and my stomach fell into a hole. For a moment I thought I was going to lose it. Sweat jumped out of my pores and the whole of my insides was shaking. I looked down at the floor and it seemed a mile down to the bottom of the stool. I sat there holding on, hoping things would normalize. It must have been some of that shit I smoked earlier, I thought. Wedo grabbed me by the shoulder and said, "You OK, man? We better head out and see if we can find Rocky." I almost jumped out of my skin. I looked at Wedo to see how he was doing. He looked fine, Wedo was drunk, but he didn't look like I felt. Ben sat hunched up to the bar, staring at his drink. I let out a scream and jump off the stool shaking my head.

"Wow man, is it getting drunk out or what!" I said, laughing. "What was that shit we were smoking earlier? I can't seem to shake it."

"Just some of the best shit south of the border, man. You have to let go of that shit in your head and go with the flow," Ben said, reaching out with those big arms, grabbing me around the shoulders and bringing me into a big bear hug. I stood there trapped in his big arms. "Stop fighting it, man."

When he let me go I had to take a deep breath to get air back into my lungs. "OK. man, I'll stop fighting it, but Wedo and me, we have to hit it and see if we can find Rocky. You still heading down south to the Yucatan to live with those Indians or are you going to hang out a while?" I asked, holding on to the stool.

"You bet, man, I'll take off tomorrow at first light, it's too drunk out to leave right now," Ben said, leaning back on the bar.

I reached over and grabbed his big beefy neck and pulled him toward me into a big hug, "OK. later then. I'll try to pick up on you tonight if this asshole skipper of mine don't kill me first," I said, looking over at Wedo. "Let's hit it my man," I said, and we started walking toward the door. I looked back at Ben and for half a second had the notion to go with him. "Fuck it, that's crazy," I said out loud, shaking my head at my own stupidly.

The sun was still up and a warm sea breeze caressed me as I stepped out on the pavement and started up the hill to the next bar.

The afternoon went by like the speed of light, one minute the sun was shinning and the next it was dark. Wedo and I sat in a dark bar, with a night-club atmosphere, talking to these two lovely ladies when all of a sudden I found myself flat on my back on the floor with a foot on my chest. Rocky was bent over me yelling, "What the fuck you doing here? You're supposed to be on the boat, goddamn it! I told you to stay on the boat. These goddamn Mexicans will steal everything that isn't nailed down."

I started to say something lame but Rocky interrupted, "Don't even open your mouth. Get your ass up and out the door." Rocky dragged me up and pushed me forward. I staggered and fell out the open doorway, laughing. The night was clear and I was standing on a hill overlooking the bay with lights emanating off the hill. What a beautiful sight, I thought, tuning Rocky out of my mind, trying to identify the *Perfect Dawn*.

"So you think this is funny, huh, mother-fucker," Rocky said, whirling me around and grabbing me by the cheek. It took a second to figure that he had his thumb under my eye, and I grabbed his forearm with both hands. "Put the hands down or I'll pop this eye right out of your fucking head, you funny motherfucker!" he said.

I put my arms down and out as if the earth were going to jump up and meet me. He walked me over to the top of the hill. "I could fuck you up real good now, couldn't I boy," Rocky said, holding me in my bent over position. I stood there waiting. "It's not so goddamn funny now, is it?" he asked, his face in close to mine. Rocky pointed out over the bay, "You see that boat out there? I want your ass back out there as fast as it takes you to get down the hill, and get a bum boat back out there. You hear what I'm saying?"

"I'm leaving now, if you'll take your finger out of my fuckin eye," I said.

Rocky let go and I staggered backward holding my eye, surprised it was still there. I started staggering down the hill muttering obscenities. I heard Rocky yell behind me, "If you don't get back to the boat, don't bother coming back."

That's the last thing I remember. The lights went out. I don't know if I passed out, or blacked out.

❧

It was like gravity had a hold on my mind and wouldn't let go. A thousand little lights seemed to be bursting out from the depths of my mind. My foot was stuck in some kind of mire and it kept pulling me down into the ooze. I lifted an eyelid, then the other popped open and gravity pulled them closed again. A shearing pain ran from my head down the back of my neck and into my shoulders. With great effort I got my eyes open again and grabbed the back of my head before it exploded.

My back was up off the floor and I was leaning on my left elbow trying desperately to grasp onto some kind of reality. Then my eyes focused and I saw a person pulling on my right boot. My left boot lay at the edge of a pool of water. The water was up to my forearm. I let out a yell and sat up, looking around. The Mexican backed off slowly, in a crouch with a slight smile on his face. I couldn't tell if he was trying to get my boot off, or pull me out of the water. Beyond him sat fifteen Mexicans on a bench along a wall. I looked up and saw bars with the blue sky above them. Then it hit me. I was in a Mexican jail. "Oh shit! Not again. Not in Mexico, goddamn it!" I said to no one in particular.

I stood up with a little difficulty, I felt like I had been run over by a big truck and maybe I had. I was in a big room, fifteen-by-thirty with a big, steel door at one end. The floor at the other end must have settled six inches, because a third of the floor was under water. There was no ceiling, just the bars, and the rain came right through. Who gives a shit if a few prisoners get saturated with water. I still had on my sweater and levis, but the jacket and bag were gone. Oh well, life goes on. I reached around and felt for my wallet; it was gone too. I sat there a minute, befuddled, then pushed myself up on my hindquarters seeking dryer ground. I stood up, dusted my pants off, and walked over to the bench. I sat alone at what I thought would be the end of the line. There was a Mexican about three feet to my left. I sat contemplating my predicament when the Mexican nudged me. I looked over at his out stretched hand. He said, "Chocolat'te." I looked at him again, trying to figure out what he was saying. He kept pushing his hand toward me saying, "Chocolat'te."

Then it hit me, chocolate candy, all right! I couldn't remember the last time I ate. I reached over and snapped off a piece, "Gracias," I said, and took a bite, then stopped and held it in my mouth wondering why it tasted so bad, no sugar. Chocolate without sugar is just not the same. In fact it was bad, but I ate it just to make him feel good, plus I was hungry, and I made a friend.

Sitting in a Mexican jail all alone and not being able to speak the language is the pits, so reaching out for a friend is the first priority.

Keys rattled in the door and everyone stood up. A jailer with a brown uniform and a night stick walked in. I stood up, too, and watched what was happening. The jailer walked through the crowd of Mexicans, answering a question here and there, kidding around with a few that had obviously been there before. Then he came up to me.

"Como se amos?" he asked, lifting the nightstick and slapping his hand with it. I stood there silent looking at him, not knowing what he said. I looked over at the Mexican, then back at the jailer.

"No comprenda," I said, hunching up my shoulders with the palms of my hands up. "I speak only a little Spanish."

"Como se amos?" he asked again. This time his voice was louder and he slapped his hand with the nightstick harder. Then he grabbed the end and held it. I felt he was going to hit me with that nightstick if I didn't come up with an answer quick. A Mexican came up to me and yelled like I was hard of hearing, "What you name?

"Pat McElroy," I said, "Yes, Pat McElroy, that's my name," I said, "I'm a fishermen."

The jailer talked to one of the Mexicans for a minute, then grunted and walked out, slamming the big door behind him. We all sat down again.

As I sat there thinking about how I was going to get out of this predicament, the steel door opened and someone said something in Spanish; everyone got up and started filing out the door. I looked around at the empty cell and decided I should follow them out. We walked down a hallway and then entered a large room. A lot of people were milling around waiting; I realized that they were family and friends of the inmates. Women would walk up, hand the inmates food and cigarettes. There was no one I knew standing out there. I was sure I looked a mess and tried to comb my hair back with my hands. We were standing in single file. As I looked around the room I became aware of a short, fat Mexican watching me. He had a pointed nose, a mustache, and small, beady eyes. He wore a brown shirt with a dark tie and dark pants. I was wondering what he found so interesting about me, when he started making his way over to me.

"You speak Spanish?" he asked me in English.

"No, I mean I speak a little. I'm off one of the shrimp boats out in the bay. We're down from Texas, blew in from that last storm." I said, wishing I had a smoke.

"Ah, Americano. You from Texas, huh, you fish off boats in bay. You have American dollars to get out of this jail?" He asked, looking at me sternly.

"I lost my wallet last night, and all my money went with it, but I still have money on the boat. If I could only get out to my boat I could get the money," I said, feeling a little braver. Maybe there was a light at the end of the tunnel.

He looked at me and said, "Hmmm." He tapped me on the shoulder with the back of his hand. "You wait here, I'll be back." He turned abruptly and walked off, disappearing into the crowd. I started to have hope that I might get out of this thing.

A few minutes later the Mexican was back, "Five hundred Pesos. That's your bail. You got five hundred Pesos on that boat?" he asked, flipping a piece of paper back and forth.

I knew that was a little high, but would have said the same thing if it had been a thousand Pesos, "Hell yes! I got the money, besides a whole boat full of fish."

"OK. You come along now," he said, and we walked out of that jail.

For a moment there I thought I was stranded in Mexico. I could only see three boats in the bay, but one looked as if it could be the *Perfect Dawn*. As we pulled away from the dock I pointed to the boat I wanted to go to. A huge pressure seemed to have grabbed me around the chest. I had to breath deep to get any air into my lungs and I realized it was fear. I started praying that the boat in the distance was the *Perfect Dawn*. Every muscle in my body was tense as I strained my eyes to see what boat was out there. There were three of us in the bum boat. I stood at the bow with the wind hitting me full on hoping we were heading toward the right boat. As we got closer the *Perfect Dawn* took on shape and I knew I was heading in the right direction. A big weight was lifted off my chest, but fear still gripped my gut. I could see someone on the back deck by now. I turned back to the man who got me out jail. "That's the one," I yelled into the wind. As we roared toward the *Perfect Dawn* I realized my attorney friend, 'if that's what he was' wasn't doing too well. He had lost his color and probably wished he was anywhere but on this little boat. The closer we got the more clearly the boat came into perspective; I could see Rocky working with the nets on the back deck. Wedo was nowhere in sight.

The little boat pulled up along side the *Perfect Dawn*, and Wedo came out of the wheelhouse and looked over at us. He gave me that knowing smile. I tossed him a line and he tied it off as I pulled myself up on the deck, "Got your ass in a sling this time, huh?" he said, his blue eyes shining, with the blond hair hanging down over them. I turned and helped my fat friend up and over the side. "What's going on with Rocky?" I asked, looking toward the back of the boat.

"I think he probably wants to kill you." I looked at Wedo to see if he was serious or not. His eyes were smiling. "Hell man, I don't know what he's thinking," he said, punching me playfully in the shoulder.

I looked down at the lawyer, pointed to the back of the boat and said, "You'll have to talk to him." I gave him a little push on his way. I went into the cabin and poured myself a cup of coffee and went down and sat on my bunk praying everything would turn out all right. I lit a smoke and waited.

It seemed an eternity before I heard the motor on the bum boat start and another couple of minutes before they pulled away from the *Perfect Dawn*. "Good! Man, damn good," I said to myself, tipping the coffee mug up for the last drink. I went up into the cabin and poured another cup of coffee, trying to get that chocolate taste out of my mouth. I was leaning up against the sink and sipping on the coffee, when Rocky came through the door, heading towards the wheelhouse.

"I was giving you an hour. You lucked out this time. Let's get that anchor up. We have to unload the fish in three hours, the *Vagabond* will carry the shrimp back to the company when they leave tomorrow," Rocky said, holding on the door frame of the wheelhouse. "OK." I said, going out the door to get the anchor ready, and breathing a lot easier.

We unloaded the shrimp that afternoon, and dropped the nets at sundown. The *Vagabond* left the next morning with our catch. Nothing more was said about Vera Cruz. We fished for another three weeks with no more mishaps.

One morning around four I stepped into the wheelhouse and said, "Everything is iced. I'm going to bed. Do you want anything before I go?"

Rocky looked up, "No, not now, but we're going to make this the last drag. And get the fuck out of here. It's time to go see momma."

"Hot damn, that's the best news I've heard all week," I said, turning and heading down to my bunk. I sat down and lit a cigarette, and started to make plans for the day we got back. But plans don't always work the way you want them to.

Didn't Look Back

CHAPTER ELEVEN

The Escape

I stepped into the cell and stopped, shocked.
The room was fifteen-by-thirty with a cement floor. It had one window
at the far end of the cell with heavy mesh screen and an aisle off to my left
with three smaller cells. Each cell had four bunks in it. There was nowhere
to step, the place was full of bodies, all Native Americans. Some were passed
out, others were sitting up against the wall with long hair hanging down over
their faces, eyes all blurry. They were every which way. One thing for sure,
they seemed to have every square inch taken up.

The jailer nudged me in and the old man followed as I tripped over the
first person, then the others started to move a little, but there was no place to
go. I was getting the idea of what a sardine felt like. I made my way along the
front wall and two Indians made room for the old man and me to sit.

Once down, I looked around at the sight with unbelieving eyes. The
bunks had three or four guys on them and the floor of the smaller cells were
full. Where in hell did all these Indians come from, I wondered. I realized
that some were still drunk. Others had been here a while and sobered up. I
figured some kind of Indian festival had taken place and they had all been
arrested for one thing or the other. I pulled out a cigarette and offered a few
around. After three or four I stopped, telling them to share.

As I watched the Indians I became aware of how close they were, in an
intimate way. A way I've never seen in the American male, myself included. I
was fascinated with them. They lay upon the bunks next to each other without a care to the closeness. A few were even brushing out one another's hair.
They seemed to genuinely care for each other and be a part of something; in

a way I was not familiar with. It made me aware of my own aloneness. Something I had not thought of before. I knew I was watching something unique. I looked over at the old man to see if he was looking at the same thing as me. He sat with his knees up against his chest, arms hanging over his knees; a cigarette hanging from his fingers. His head looking down at the floor between his legs, he missed it all. The only thing that he could think of was his self, and how to get out of this predicament. I couldn't begrudge the man his self pity. Being in jail is never any fun, but I'd been the driver and now I was behind bars for drunk driving. I started thinking about Wedo and life's little tricks that seem to play themselves out.

ℭ

Five days after leaving Vera Cruz the *Perfect Dawn* was back in Port Isabel. Wedo and I unloaded and cleaned the boat. I packed what little gear I had, and put it in the fish house, then told Rocky I would be heading for California whenever my check was ready, in the meantime I needed a draw to go over to Boy's Town and say goodbye to Maria Lana. Rocky and I had talked about California on the trip back, he had tried talking me out of it, but my mind was made up. The article I had read about the Beat's in Venice Beach was on my mind again, I felt I had to get there before the summer started.

I met Jim a couple hours later at the Mexican cafe and we had a few beers, then Wedo showed and we were off. "Let's get Fucked Up," I said, with a big smile, while rubbing my hands together.

Two days later I was sitting in a small cantina trying to force a couple of eggs down. The cantina had a short counter with three stools, and two tables. A small, fat Mexican woman was cooking behind the counter, wearing a flowery, blue dress that had seen better days. The place smelled of grease and stale beer; a great smell if you can get a beer down quick. I was suffering a bad hangover when Billy Dee walked in and saw me in my misery, "Those huervos any good?" He asked, pulling up a chair and sitting down.

"Yeah, hot as a firecracker," I said, tipping a bottle of beer and chugging it to wash everything down. "Where you been, haven't seen you in a couple of months," I said, reaching for a cigarette. My head was starting to feel a little better.

"I went to Florida for a while to see my folks, then to Mississippi to see some friends. I got back a few days ago. I'll be out of money in a while so

I guess its time to go back to work," he said. "Oh, by the way, I seen Wedo over in Brownsville and he told me to tell you he went back to the boat."

"Yeah, the chicken-hearted, I knew he'd head back pretty quick. Six weeks on a boat and all you get off is two days. That's bullshit. Rocky wanted to head back out in two days and I'll bet Rocky don't sober up for two more days. And another bet I'll make is that they don't get out till next Monday, but that's not my problem any more. I'm not working on the boat now, so it's none my business."

"You're not working for Rocky anymore, what in hell you going to do now, get another boat?" He asked, then looked over at the woman behind the counter and said, "Two chicken tacos with beans and a Carta Blanka, please."

"Hell no, I'm off for California in a few days. Say man, why not come with me? We'll have a blast. We'll hitchhike up through Denver and see the Rocky Mountains, then on to L.A. and Venice Beach. Maybe head up to San Francisco."

"Hell, man, I got a couple hundred bucks, that's it. By the time I get out of Boy's Town I'll be broke. No man, I don't want to travel without money."

"Shit, man, I'm in the same boat, but I do have a couple hundred at the office, plus a few bucks on me. By the time I get out of Dodge, I'll be flat." I said, taking another hit off the bottle. I lit a cigarette.

"Besides my woman hasn't seen me in a hell of a long time, and we have a lot of lovin' to catch up on. I'm tired of travelin', that's all I been doing lately. All I want to do now is drink, make love, and have a good time."

"I hear ya man, I'm doing the same thing, but I'm still going to California, money or no money. If I don't leave now, I'll be talking about going out west next year, and I ain't having none a that." The lady brought over the tacos and beer. I watched Billy Dee eat the tacos for a minute, then picked up my bottle as I stood up and took a long drink. "Well if you change your mind, let me know, I'm going back to the room to see if Maria's up, so I can get rid of the rest of this hangover. She's got the cure, man." I set the bottle down. "Catch ya later," I said, heading for the door.

"Yeah, later, man, and don't hold your breath waiting for me to go out to California with ya," Billy Dee said between mouthfuls of taco. I waved as I strolled out the door.

❧

Six days later I slammed the door on the old pickup truck I'd been riding in and said thanks for the lift. I had grabbed a ride in Boy's Town from another fisherman who was heading back to Port Isabel. Maria Lana was hard on my mind. I hadn't said anything to her about leaving for California. I was feeling guilty and couldn't shake it, but I knew there would be a big scene if I said anything. Mexican women are hot-blooded creatures when they are in love with a man. There was never any doubt that she would have shot me if she found me with another woman. She might not have killed me, but she would make sure I was dammed sorry I played around.

One evening, late in the night, Maria pulled a pistol out of her drawer and showed it to me, then pointed it at me and said, "You no fuckee around on me or else, Boom, Boom." We laughed, but we both knew she was serious. I loved Maria in my own way, even whores have feelings, and she had a lot of feeling for me, but I was heading out West and that was that. I'd have Rocky or Wedo tell her I was gone whenever they went back to Boy's Town.

Once in Port Isabel I stepped into the Mexican cantina and looked around till I saw Billy Dee sitting at a table looking out over the bay. The place had windows on three walls and a bar at the back. Five tables sat in middle of the floor. I walked around the tables and sat down next to Billy Dee, and yelled out to mamma-sita for two more beers. I was down to my last two dollars and glad I hadn't picked up the rest of my money yet.

"Que Pa-so, Billy, so, you beat me back, huh. I had a hard time getting away from Maria Lana, one more time, that's all that woman knows. I'm such a lover I can't stand myself," I said, laughing. Billy kept looking at me without saying a word. "What's happening, man? You look like you just got out of church."

"I take it you haven't heard about Wedo?" He said, looking down at his glass of beer.

I stopped laughing and looked at him. Billy Dee didn't say anything. "Well, what's going on, man?"

"They found Wedo floating in the bay last night, deader than a doornail. He was all bloated up from the water and scraping on the bottom of the boats. They figured he had been in the water for about three days." Billy Dee stopped talking to let that sink in.

"What the fuck you talking about," I said. "I just talked to him a couple days ago. He can't be dead." The tears shot into my eyes with a force that amazed me. "Are they sure it's Wedo, maybe it was someone that looked like him," I said, hoping.

"No, no it's him all right. Rocky went down and identified the body this morning."

I slammed my fist down on the table and ran outside wiping the tears from my eyes and walked a block down the road trying to keep from crying. My whole head felt like it would explode. I took some deep breaths and started feeling a little better. I turned and started back toward the cantina, I needed to find out the rest of the story.

Billy was still sitting there when I walked through the door. Two beers sat on the table untouched. I walked over and sat down, then drank half the beer that was sitting in front of me. "Well, did somebody kill him or what? I can't believe he just fell off the boat."

"Nobody knows. His body was so banged up from scraping on the bottom of the boats; it's hard to tell what happened. They're calling it an accident," Billy Dee said, still staring out the window.

I knew Rocky had the ability to kill Wedo if he was mad enough, but knowing the two of them like I did, it was doubtful Rocky would do anything, besides he treated Wedo like he was a stern father most of the time.

"Where's Rocky now?" I asked, picking up the bottle and drinking the rest of the beer.

"Him and Norm went over to the undertaker's to make arrangements for the body to be shipped up north to his parents. They should be back any time now.

"Well shit, I've got to go over and get my check and grab a shower. I'll stop by the boat and see if he's there," I went over to the bar and paid for the beers, then looked back and waved as I stepped out the door.

∽

They cashed my check at the Perfect Office, so, with money in hand I started back to the bar. Rocky wasn't at the boat so I figured he would be at the bar. I took my raingear and put it on the back of the boat. I definitely was not going to carry that heavy shit all the way to California. The next guy that came along could have it. That lightened my load quite a bit since I'd lost most of my stuff down in old Mexico. I still had my heavy turtleneck sweater that I was wearing and a chalecko; a colorful, wool vest. If it didn't get too cold I'd be alright.

The bar was half full when I entered from the side door. Rocky sat at a table by himself in the back just staring into a glass of beer. I pulled up a chair and sat down, then yelled over to the bartender for a couple of beers. Rocky looked up at me with droopy eyes and said, "I take it, you've heard already what happened to Wedo?"

"I heard it, but I can't believe it," I said, throwing a couple of dollars out on the table for the beers. "Are you sure it was him. Billy Dee said, he was all bloated and scraped from the bottom of the boats. I just can't believe he would fall off a boat by himself. He must of gotten into a fight or something and somebody dumped him into the bay."

The barmaid brought the two beers over to the table and started to take a dollar. I laid my hand on hers and said, "Get Billy Dee and Norm and those other guys a drink. In fact get them all a drink. I'm the last of the big spenders, I guess."

"Well there's nobody jumping out saying they did it, is there? Anyway he's just as dead," Rocky said, lifting his glass and taking a drink.

I took a cigarette out of my pocket and lit it. "The body is being shipped up north then. I guess there isn't much I can do. You know how bad I feel about this don't you? I loved the guy," I said, taking a drag off the smoke and inhaling it deep into the lungs, needing too feel the pressure; then letting the smoke out slowly.

"You still going out to California? I'm in need of a rig man now. It's your job if you want it. You might as well hang out a couple months and get yourself some good money before you head out," Rocky said. "You'll just get there and be broke if you leave now."

"Naw, I gotta go now, it's my destiny. If I hang out a couple of months I probably still won't have the money. There is never enough money for what a guy wants, so I have to be able to make it without the money." I looked over at Billy Dee and said, "You're sure you don't want to make a run to California with me? I'm taking off in a few minutes."

"No, I'm broke and I'm not traveling without money. But maybe I'll catch up with you next year," Billy Dee said with a big smile. "Hey Maria," he said, waving his arm at the barmaid "Bring over some more beers. Maybe we can get Pat drunk enough to change his mind."

"No way, my man, one more and that's it, I'm out of here." I said with more confidence then I felt.

We drank a few more beers and said our goodbyes. Then I hit the road.

It's a thousand miles up to El Paso and it took a bunch of short rides to get there. Wedo's death hung on me like an invisible veil for the next couple days. I got drunk in El Paso. Three days later I was in New Mexico.

❦

I was standing alongside the road in Albuquerque, N.M. with my thumb out. The town stretched out as far as the eye could see. Businesses on both sides of Route 66: gas stations, restaurants, bars. New businesses and parking lots were being built along the highway.

Route 66 was jammed with autos; it was the main route between New York and Los Angeles. People were on the move. A half mile ahead I could see a large dust cloud and big machines moving back and forth; highway construction. All of a sudden a big green Buick pulled off the road. I waited for the dust to settle down and saw a small head through the rear window, then I ran toward the car. The dust got into my throat making me cough. I opened the door and jump in. The old man looked smaller than he actually was; he was about five foot ten inches. The old guy looked as if someone had poured him into the car; the clothes looked as if they had not seen a wash in a week. He had the beginnings of a gray, beard. The blue eyes were blood-shot and glassy. I feared they might fall out, if he opened them any farther. "You have a driver's license? he asked.

"Yes," I said.

"Well, come around this side and you can drive. I'm beat," he said, sliding over toward the passenger side of the car.

I got out and walked around to the driver's side and got in. "How far you going?" I asked, starting the big Buick while listening to the engine purr. This is some kind of power, I thought, putting the car into gear and heading out onto the highway.

"L.A.," he said. He thought a minute then he said, "You drink beer?"

"Sure, I'll take one and I'm heading out to L. A. myself," I said, looking over at him as he took a ten dollar bill out of his pocket and passed it over to me. I took it and asked, "What's this?

"Pull over at the next liquor store and get three six-packs of beer and pint of vodka and maybe some bologna and bread."

I stopped and picked up the stuff and came out and got into the car, cracking a beer as I sat down.

By the time we got to Arizona I was into the third six-pack. I'd just driven through Holbrook, and was heading out of town when I looked up into my rear view mirror and saw the red flashing lights. I looked down at my speed, it read sixty. I pulled over to the side of the road. They said I was doing eighty through town and drunk besides. I didn't believe it but there I was, sitting in jail.

Monday morning we all went to court. "Ninety days," the judge said, and they took me back to the county jail. The last thing the old man said as he went through the door was, "Don't worry about a thing, my boy. I'll pay your bail and we'll be on our way."

Two hours later I knew who was on their way and it sure as hell wasn't me.

The judge had let most of the Indians out, so all of a sudden there was a lot of room in the tank, but that didn't last. By noon, fifteen of us were being marched across the lawn of the court house with only one guard. The court house was a three-story, red brick building on the main street, Route 66. The county jail was on the third floor of the court house. We marched three abreast around the back of the court house to a small building, and into the basement, which was the city jail. The upper floor housed the police station.

The place I found myself in was not like a normal jail. It was a large room, with two rows of pillars running the length of the building. Beds were set up at right angles to the concrete block walls; all around the perimeter of the room. A few beds scattered around the center, dormitory style. Most of the beds had a bare mattress folded in half on top. All my cellmates were Indian, so I didn't say much, I just followed their lead. I found a bunk and threw the mattress out and found a sheet and a blanket, then made up the bed and sat down to smoke a cigarette as I'd looked around the room. Up near the ceiling were windows that opened from the top and pulled out and away from the wall, with heavy mesh screens on the outside. Two picnic tables sat in the center of the room.   Three men at the far end of the room were moving beds up close together. They climbed up on the head-rail pulling on a window over-head. The window popped opened and everybody got excited, talking among themselves. Somebody on the outside had pulled the wire mesh away from the window and started passing bags through the opening. I saw two half-gallons of wine come through and a carton of cigarettes and I thought I saw two hypodermic needles. Now what would Indians want with hypodermic needles?

I had just finished taking a shower and was getting into my pants when I heard someone say, "Dinner," and everyone started toward the door. "What's going on?" I asked a young Indian standing next to his bunk. He was about eighteen, slim build, with jeans and a cowboy shirt. His hair was shorter than most of the other Indians. When he smiled, it was a friendly smile, so I took to him right off the top. "Its dinner time," he said. They'll march us down to the diner down the street."

I threw a shirt on and ran to get in line. Once outside we got four abreast and walked down the street then crossed the lawn over to the main street and headed in a westerly direction. Most businesses were closed this time of the evening, it was after five. The traffic had slowed down for the day. Several cars were still parked along the curb. We passed a small park on our right with a couple of trees and sidewalks running over to the next street. Three picnic benches, no lawn just sand. We started across the street to the next block. I was at the back of the line and saw two Indians up front take off running. I looked around to see who was going to chase them. We had two sheriff's deputies walking beside us, but they did nothing, they didn't even quit talking. There were about thirty of us when we left; now there were twenty-eight. I looked over at the young Indian walking beside me, "What's that all about?" I asked. "It's just desert out there. They'll pick them up in no time."

"It'll be dark in a bit and they'll make their way back to the reservation under the cover of darkness. The deputies will pick them up the next time they raise hell in town. It's a big game they play. The sheriff can't go on the reservation. It has its own police, so the city cops wait for em to come back into town. They know they'll get them sooner or later.

"Oh," I said, turning that over in my mind.

We marched down to the restaurant and filed inside. The place was empty. Five booths lined the wall on the right as we came through the door, and we filled them. The room was long and narrow with a counter on our left that ran most of the length of the room. The waitress brought out the food fast and furious slamming it down in front of us, wishing that we were anywhere but there; then hurried away for fear of catching something horrible. The meal consisted of hamburger, mashed potatoes and green beans. I ate mine with a vengeance for fear she might come and take it back. I looked over at the young Indian who seemed to be staying close to me for some reason, "Now that's some good food. Those guys who took off should have waited till after they ate. It would have gotten them through the night."

He just smiled with his mouth full. On the way back to the city jail another Indian took off. It looks pretty easy, I thought.

A steady influx of inmates kept the population at about thirty. And each time we were marched over to the restaurant, one or two Indians would take off. On the forth night, after we had eaten, I positioned myself on the inside next to the buildings, and up front, ready to take flight if the opportunity presented itself. As we started walking back to the jail, I looked around to see where the deputies were. They were a quarter of the way up the line talking as usual. I noticed the young Indian was behind me, in the second line. He gave me a smile as if he knew what was on my mind.

We came to the end of the block and were about to cross the street when I made my move. I stepped out of line, ducking behind the first building and running for the end of the block. I swung around the last building and headed west. I didn't know where I was going, but west was the way I wanted to head. I wanted to get out into the desert as quick as possible, away from the houses and the lights. I cut across the street and into a vacant lot. All of a sudden I realized someone was chasing me. I looked back to see the young Indian on my tail. He had decided to come along. I didn't give it that much thought; I was just glad that it wasn't a deputy ready to snatch me up. I kept running and the houses thinned out. The fear left me and I slowed to a quick trot but kept moving fast. I didn't want to get caught now, with this taste of freedom that I felt. We had gotten into the dunes and were staying on the north side of Route 66. I knew I had to make it at least twenty miles to be out of the county.

"Wait, wait awhile, I can't go any farther."

I looked back and the young Indian had plopped himself down on the ground. I came to a halt and looked around to be sure we were alone. Then dropped down to my knees and sat back on the side of a large dune with my arms upon my knees, letting my head fall between the knees.

"I thought all you Indians could run for miles. What's the deal?" I asked, taking in large gulps of air.

"That was the old Indians. I'm a modern day Indian. We don't run so much. Besides, it'll be dark soon," he said, falling back into the sand, landing on his elbows.

After my wind returned I lit a cigarette and asked, "What made you take off after me?"

"I was going to run at the same place, but you ran first so I had to follow. After a while I will head north up to the reservation. You should come with me. No police on the reservation."

I thought about it for a minute, either this kid has taken a liken to me or he's afraid to run alone in the dark. "I'll think about it. You got a name? Mine's Pat," I said, pushing myself up to my feet.

"My name's Russell," he said, looking up at me.

136

"It's time to get the hell out of here, Russell" I turned and started running through the sand.

I've heard of darkness falling, but out on the desert it fell like a blanket. Russell and I did a lot of stumbling at first, but with all the stars and a half-moon, my eyes became accustomed to the dark and we were able to move along quickly. It was close to midnight when we came across an old pickup about three hundred feet from the main house. We had seen the house lights for a long time, but on the desert with its cold air, the lights were a hell of a lot farther than a person would think.

The pickup was a 1940s dodge that had been sitting a long time. I opened the creaking door slowly so as not to make too much noise. I didn't want to wake any dogs and get them to barking. The last thing I wanted to see was old Farmer John coming out with a shotgun and shooting up the night. Russell on the other side just grabbed the door and pulled it open. The creaking was loud enough to wake the dead.

"Hey, stop that noise," I yelled in a whisper. I looked around and waited for a dog to start yelping. Russell froze where he was at. Everything was quiet so we climbed into the front seat of the pickup. I sat there for a minute with the door ajar, it felt good not to be running, "We must of come twenty miles," I said, reaching for a smoke and lighting it.

"No, maybe ten miles. Joseph is just down the road."

I sat smoking, watching the stars. There seemed to be billions of them almost as if you could reach out and touch them.

"Ten miles still ain't bad. Joseph – is that a town or a person?" I asked, looking over at Russell. He was snoring lightly. I flipped the butt out the side door and lay back and closed my eyes.

I awoke to the sound of a rooster crowing somewhere in the distance. The sun was up and it was cold as hell. Russell had fallen over into my lap and I had dropped over on his back. That's how we slept the night out. He sat up with his arms crossed, rubbing his elbows.

"I'm frozen, why did you wake me up? I was so warm."

"You used me as a blanket. I've gotta get moving and get out of this county before they start a real search for me. You, they might not care about, but I don't know how they feel about me. I'm still going to move it on down the line," I said, reaching for a smoke. "Man, what I wouldn't do for a cup of coffee." Then it hit me, my wallet and what little money I had was still back at that jail. "Goddamn it," I said, "I left my wallet at that jail."

"I guess you could've stopped and picked it up as we left," Russell said, stomping his feet on the ground, trying to keep warm. "I'm going up to the reservation from here. You should think about coming with me for a week or two. Then be on your way. They will pick you up in no time as soon as you start hitch-hiking out on the highway."

"I have a better plan. I'll make my way over to Winslow, and catch a fright train heading for L.A. They have a big freight yard there, it should be easy. Anyway, that's what I want to do," I said, taking a drag off the smoke and looking out over the desert, wondering how hard it would be to stay out of sight from the highway.

Russell walked over and stuck out his hand, "I think you should come with me, but have a good trip. We will remember each other from this day on because of the run through the desert for most of a night, and our great escape." I took his hand looking at him and knew I had a friend here in this Indian kid.

"Most people don't break out of jail every day, I said, shaking his hand. "You're right, it was a good run. I didn't know I had it in me and I hope that's the last jail I have to break out of." I watched as he turned and took off to the north. I ground out the butt of the cigarette and started off west.

I worked my way over to Winslow and found the freight yard. Winslow was a long desert town, maybe a couple thousand people. The town didn't appeal to me much; some people love the desert, but all I see is sand and sagebrush and when the wind blows it's like being sandblasted. The sand gets into the eyes, ears, and hair, and it makes a person feel crusty all over.

The more I thought about catching the freight, the more I didn't like the idea. All I had was the clothes I was wearing, a chalecko, the wool sweater I got down in Mexico and a pair of jeans. I would look like a coal miner when I got off the train.

I skirted around the yard, which was a half-mile around. There were boxcars as far as the eye could see. Most were hooked up to each other just sitting there. A lot of action was going on – big engines, two or three, sometimes four, hooked together. They were being backed up or pulled forward, hooking on to long lines of boxcars moving them from track to track. Cars would sit waiting for the big engines to pick them up and head for a final destination. Route 66 was just a stone's throw away, and maybe I was out of the county.

I thought why not, what the hell. So, I walked out into the open and crossed over a ditch to the highway and walked down to the crossroads. I still wanted to ride the rails but that would wait for another day.

I wasn't there five minutes when I saw a patrol car coming down the road. He slowly pulled off the highway and drove toward me. I just stood there, standing in the middle of the desert with no place to run. "Ah shit," I said to myself. The deputy stepped out of the car. "McElroy, get in the back," he said as he opened the door. I got in the back and sat there, part of me glad it was over and part of me wishing I had made it on down the road. I knew that at some point I would have had to come back and clean this thing up; now was as good a time as any. Besides I wanted my wallet and papers that they still held at the jail.

The cop turned and put his arm up on the seat and gave me a big smile, "You made it quite a ways but you still had a long way to go to get out of this county. You really fucked up this time. You've set yourself up for five years," he said, giving me a wink of the eye. The patrol car pulled out into the highway, making a U-turn.

"Five years, what the fuck! Are you crazy? How could I get five years?"

"That's what they give prisoners for escape," he said, stepping on the accelerator.

By the time we got to the edge of town the cop was doing eighty. I sat in the back thinking about five years. They can't give me five years, I was only doing ninety days for Christ sakes, I thought, pulling out a cigarette. "Is it all right if I smoke?" I asked, putting the cigarette between my lips. He looked at me through the rear view mirror with smiling eyes, "Sure, go ahead," he said. He knew he had me.

I sat there thinking that I should have gone to the reservation with Russell, damn it. Well, next time I would.

There was no next time. They put me back in the county jail and kept me there. Two weeks I sat waiting to go to court, or something. But nothing happened, and then one day my name was called. I walked up to the door and the guard said, "If we let you out, how fast can you get out of town?"

"Hell, I'll move so fast you won't even see my feet hit the ground," I said with a big smile. Fifteen minutes later I was hitch-hiking out of town and again I didn't get to eat dinner, but that was no big thing. I had my wallet with a few bucks in it and I felt great to be out in the open.

Well, I didn't get out of town that fast. I stood at the edge of town trying to get a ride, but nothing was happening. I could see a café a quarter mile down the road and it was starting to get dark, so I walked on down to grab a bite to eat. The café sat fifty feet off the highway, with six cars in front, nothing else around.

As I started in I noticed a movement in the back of the car I was passing. I looked in and saw this big white cat with dark spots pawing the window. Its long tail had curled at the end, moving slowly back and forth. The tail moved like a snake under a spell. I jumped back, my heart pounding a mile a minute. I stood there looking at it and laughed, the fear receding. I didn't know what the hell kind of cat it was; but it too small to be a leopard. It was three times bigger then any normal cat. After a while it laid down in the back seat. I shook my head thinking some people are just plain crazy, and went into the café.

I stepped down from the café steps with a paper cup full of hot coffee. I felt better having had a hamburger and some fries. The car with the cat was still there. The cat was now in the front seat pawing at the side window as if he wanted to talk to me. I tapped on the window with my finger nails as I walked by. I found a place about a hundred feet west of the restaurant and set my coffee down on the ground and lit a cigarette. It was dark by this time and getting a ride after dark gets a little more difficult.

I hadn't been there five minutes when a car from the restaurant started pulling out. I jumped up from where I had been kneeling and got my thumb out. The dark colored Ford sedan pulled up slowly and came to a stop. I opened the door and looked in at the driver. A man in his early thirties, wearing glasses with short blond hair. Sure enough the cat was in the back seat. I looked at the cat as if maybe I'd wait for the next ride. "She's harmless," the driver said. "Well she's not harmless, but she won't hurt you. Come on ahead and get in."

I slid into the seat and closed the door. "It's that not harmless part that worries me," I said, looking back the cat. "What kind of cat is she anyway?"

"She's an ocelot. I got her down in Mexico; they run wild down through Mexico and South America. She's a good girl, aren't you Susie," he said, rubbing the side of her head. "She'll whip any three dogs, believe me," he said, pulling out onto the highway. "How far you going?" he asked.

"Right out to L.A." I said, "How about you?"

"I'm going over to Needles, California, so you got a ride that far anyway," he said.

"Hey, that's great, I can be in L.A. by tomorrow," I said. I felt a pat on the back of my head. I looked around at the ocelot. She sat there looking at me as if to say, "Who me?" After the third time I started getting used to it.

"She likes your long hair," the man said, reaching in his shirt pocket for a smoke. Want one? he asked.

"No thanks, I got my own," I said, pulling out a smoke. Lately everybody was switching over to filters, so I figured if it was going to kill ya, you might as well smoke what you liked.

"What are you going to do out in L.A.?" he asked, opening his side window to let out the smoke. I did the same, then leaned back on the seat and got a pat on the back of the head.

"I thought I would go out and check out the beatniks in Venice, maybe go up to San Francisco and see what's happening up there. Try to feel the beat of California and its people. Besides the weather is a lot warmer than Ohio," I said, pat on the back of the head.

"How do you like our new President?" the man asked.

For the next five hours we talked about everything, from President Kennedy, to civil rights, to communism, Marxism, Socialism. We talked about philosophers, past and present; where the country was going, and where it might go with the new president.

We talked about life, and how to live it, about chasing the holy dollar, or being satisfied with what a person needs.

When I got out of the car my brain was about to explode, I was so energized. All I could do was walk back and forth on the highway. It was after midnight. There was so much to learn that I didn't know and life to experience.

Fifteen minutes passed and I was still pacing back and forth when a big semi-truck passed then came to halt a hundred feet down the road. I started running for fear he'd change his mind. I reached up, pulling the door open and climbed up and into the cab. A skinny little guy was driving this big rig. He sat there pouring a cup of coffee till I got seated then maneuvered the big rig out on the highway, "There's a cup on the hook behind your head if you want a cup," he said, "How far you going?"

"Right to the beach in L.A.," I said, looking around for the cup, it was behind the door. A sleeping compartment the width of the truck was behind the front seats. A dark curtain was pulled closed. He had a baseball cap cocked on the back of his head and a checkered shirt. A dozen lights from the dash glowed green and blues all through the cab.

There was a C.B. radio over his head and a speaker at the end of a cord that hung on the side of the radio. He got her rolling down the road about fifty and into the last gear. "I picked you up so you could help me stay awake. It's against company rules, but sometimes you have to break the rules to get the job done. I'm on my way to Santa Barbara. I can take you to Ventura, that's about sixty miles north of Santa Monica. That's probably where you want to go. Think you can do that?" He shifted down as we started up a long slope.

"You bet. I'm good at staying awake on long hauls," I said, not telling him that I'd been lying around in a jail for the last couple of weeks.

He got into a straightaway and put the gear into high. Leaning forward, he grabbed a tin foil pack off the dash. "Want to split a benny with me? He asked, unfolding the foil.

"A benny, what the hell's a benny?" I asked, watching him open the foil.

"Benzedrine, it helps you stay awake," he said, taking a little, purple, heart-shaped pill out of the pack and breaking it in half. He handed part of it over to me. I sat looking at that little half a heart pill in the palm of my hand, "You think this will be enough to keep me awake through the rest of the night?" I asked, not believing him.

"You bet, yes sir'ree little buddy, that'll do the trick," he said, giving me this big fiendish smile in that green and blue light coming off the dash.

So I tossed it into my mouth, and drank some coffee to wash it down, "We'll see," I said, watching the road. We seemed to be climbing again. I started telling him about the ride I had before I got this ride, what we had talked about, and before you know it he and I were talking about the same stuff, only different.

I became aware of the sound of the engine, it seemed to be all around me, then it seemed to become a part of me. I could feel the night passing outside with dots of light off in the distance. I could feel the truck working its way up over the hills and flying down into the valleys. We talked through the night it seemed, but the night kept on going and still I talked. I had this overwhelming urge to talk, any feeling of sleepiness had left long ago. I felt wonderful.

We were coming off a mountain somewhere near San Bernardino. As we started around this long curve, the whole Los Angeles basin came into view. My heart started beating faster, and my breathing stopped for a minute. The lights extended as far west and south as the eye could see. The north was blocked by a mountain range. I looked out over the basin and my heart felt as if it would burst. Then it hit me, I was holding my breath. "Wow," was all I could get out.

On and on we rolled down the mountain, the sound of the engine running through my veins and the talk never ceasing. Down to the valley floor and through all the small towns that are sprinkled around Los Angeles. The driver pulled the big truck over to the side of the road when we arrived in Ventura. We sat there talking for another five minutes. He gave me directions on where to go when I got to Santa Monica. But I knew where I wanted to go: Venice Beach.

Didn't Look Back

CHAPTER TWELVE

California

I came walking out of the liquor store with a six-pack of Coors in one hand and a pack of Pall Malls in the other. It was ten on a Saturday night in Los Angeles. A Sambo's pancake house was on one corner and shops were opened all down the street. I stood on the opposite corner by the liquor store. Traffic was moving smoothly down Venice Boulevard. It was as bright as day with all the lights.

I opened the door of the 1955 Chevy and stepped in, putting the beer in the back seat. Jeff was in the driver's seat holding a beer in his right hand; the left was on the steering wheel. Jeff was tall and lean, six foot, a hundred and eighty pounds, wearing white t-shirt and Levis. He set the beer between his thighs and turned the key, the engine came alive. I opened a can as he backed out and slowly moved into the traffic.

Jeff had been in Los Angeles for about ten months. He was a lineman for the telephone company. He came from Edmonds, Oklahoma. I asked him one time if he could repair my phone for me. He said, "I just work on lines." Jeff and I had met in Texas ten months earlier. He came out to Los Angeles to see his sister and get away from fishing. I was hoping he might get me on with the phone company. I hit town two days ago, and we had been partying ever since.

"Well what say we head down to the beach and see what's happening, maybe pick up on a couple of chicks? Ya never know, we could get lucky," Jeff said.

"Sure, why not," I said, bending over and turning the knob on the radio, looking for some good rock music. I took a long pull on the beer as Jeff stopped for a red light. "Now, will ya look as this," Jeff said, directing his head towards the car next to us.

I leaned forward to look past him, and two fine looking women were smiling back at me. I couldn't believe our luck. The next instant they were gone. "What the hell you waiting for man! Let's go after them," I said stomping on the floor and jumping up and down.

Jeff put her in low and tromped the gas. In less then a minute we were doing seventy, their tail lights getting closer. We slowed and came to a stop at the next light, and there they sat, one blonde, the other brunette, both with big smiles. The one closest to us lifted herself off the seat and put her breasts up against the window, and then we were alone. I watched their taillights leave in the distance. "What in hell is that about?"

"I don't know, but we're sure as hell going to find out," Jeff said as the speedometer climbed to sixty.

The girls pulled over in front of us and slowed, then made a right turn, we were right behind them driving a little slower now. We followed a few blocks and when they made a left, we were right on their tail. Four more blocks and they turned into a drive and disappeared. We followed them in behind an apartment building and found ourselves in a parking lot. The girls jumped out of their car running and laughing towards the building and disappeared into a dark hallway.

Jeff pulled into a parking space and let the engine idle. "What do you think of that?"

I took a long pull on the beer and said, "Give it a minute, we'll see what happens."

I stuck a cigarette between my lips and lit it, listening, then I heard it: a sound like horse's hoofs. As I listened, it became more distinct and I knew it was stomping boots. I could hear chains rattling against the floor. "Ambush!" I yelled.

Jeff had wasted no time; the car was already backing out. I started rolling up the window on my side, looking over at the dark hallway. All of a sudden it was alive with men. There must have been fifteen or twenty of them. Chains started hitting the car, people all over the place beating on the windows. My window was about halfway up when I heard, "You son of bitch," and a fist came through the window. There was an arm attached to it. He had just missed my head, so I grabbed it and held on, the car picking up momentum. I could feel the guy struggling and hitting the side of the car as we went around the corner. We picked up more speed as the car straightened out, then I let go, knowing that this guy was going to be feeling bad when he hit the dirt. "I'll bet he don't pull that shit for a while," I said, as Jeff whipped out into the street at thirty-five. I looked back, and there were still guys running after the car, screaming with their arms in the air. Jeff went through the first stop sign, both of us laughing hysterically. At the second one he stopped, "I guess it's safe to stop here," he said, wiping the tears away from his eyes.

"Don't wait too long, the last time I looked those bastards were still running after us. Man was that close or what? The way they came outta that hallway I thought there was no end to 'em. I knew we were going to get murdalized." I reached over the seat for a couple of beers and asked, "Do ya want one?"

"Hell yes, after that shit, I need six."

I popped them open and dropped a can between my thighs and handed him one. "Well ol' Betsy-girl got us out of that one," I said, kissing the dash. The car shot forward, heading for the boulevard.

Once out on the boulevard we pulled into a gas station to check the outside of the car for damage. There were a few small dents in the side and a couple in the trunk lid. "I guess I'll have to live with it," Jeff said.

"Man, just think, that could have been our heads. Besides, it gives the car character," I said. "Let's mosey on down to the beach and see what's on the scene."

We pulled back out into the traffic as Jeff lit a joint, grabbing all the smoke that came off the lit end with his nostrils, and held it down in his lungs. His lungs wanted to expel it, but he kept it down, snorting. He handed the joint to me and I took a hit.

"Man, that's some good dope," he said.

I didn't say anything to that. Smoking pot was just a social thing with me after having had that bad trip down in Mexico.

"Man, I'm sure glad you showed up. Just think, I'd still be cooped up in that little room at my sister's, smoking this good dope instead of being out here on the streets of L.A. where anything can happen to a poor white boy like myself," Jeff said.

"Shit man, I'll bet you ain't been laid since Mexico," I said, handing him the joint.

"That's true, but I've been alive."

"You can't call that living, man, working all day and staying in a little room the rest of the time. A man needs pussy or his brain deteriorates all to hell."

He made a right at the light, went down to Windward, then he turned left down to the beach.

We parked the car and walked down the street. There were houses on both sides of the street; within feet of each other, tightly packed. The street ended at a wide alley that ran north to Santa Monica and south to the canals. It ran behind the shops. During the day loading trucks used the road, or anybody trying to get to the beach. We crossed over to the corner. Two hundred feet down a slight hill was the boardwalk.

❧

The Venice North coffee shop sat on one corner of the alley. Across the street was a three-story building, a tattoo parlor was on the first floor, a vegetable market took up the front and spilled out into boardwalk. As we walked down the slope, Deana's Pizza Parlor was on our right. Three big windows covered the wall, each one larger then the previous one as they went down the slope. The boardwalk was fifty feet across. A covered picnic area was on the west side of the boardwalk with two tables inside and a three-foot high brick wall around the perimeter.

A big, black guy with a large beard was beating on a huge conga drum. A tall black man with slim features and a goatee played the flute; a French beret sat on the side of his head. A white guitar player and a red-haired girl playing the bongos rounded out the players. Four other people stood around shaking to the beat of the small band. A gallon of burgundy wine was sitting on the table for anybody to take a drink. The fog was undulating back and forth making the small group look ominous.

As I looked north, lights spilled out of the pizza house and the other businesses on the front. Another vegetable stand was next door, a Chinese take-out a couple of doors down. I could see a liquor store a little farther down the walk, but most of the light came from Pacific Ocean Park; a huge amusement park a half mile away. It had a rollercoaster, Ferris wheel, even an aquarium for large fish, one of the biggest on the West Coast. Even at midnight there were several people walking on the front. The parking lot across the walk was almost empty.

To the south, the only light was from the light posts set every hundred feet for a mile or so. Not too many businesses, a bar or two. The center of Venice was three-quarters of a mile south. With the fog moving in on the darkness, the surf pounding on the beach, it seemed an eerie stretch.

Double doors opened at the corner of the Pizza Parlor. Jeff and I stood smoking our cigarettes and watching the people inside. I didn't know a soul in this town so I left it up to Jeff to try and score some grass and bennies. Three young guys stood out front, near us, checking out the action. They probably didn't know any more then we did.

"One way to tell the locals from the tourists, the ones with the clear eyes are the tourists, the locals are the fucked-up ones," Jeff said.

"I'm hip," I said starting into the pizza house, trying to look cool. I turned and walked back to Jeff, getting up close. "Try and get the purple-hearted bennies if you can, man. That was the best high I ever had."

"I'll try, but like I said, I've never seen 'em."

"Well, whatever," I said, and headed on in.

The pizza room was huge, thirty-by-fifty, windows running down the right side and the front. The wall to my left was solid white. Two pool tables were up front, six picnic tables were behind, then a counter. A small man with thick glasses, a large nose and balding head was taking orders. Both pool tables were in use. There were benches along both walls.

Three black men stood along the wall to my left, dressed in dark suits, talking and watching the pool games. Two women with short dresses were playing on the first table. A thin, black guy with big, dark sunglasses, a black turtleneck and a large round medallion hanging from his neck, was taking a shot. A striking brunette with long straight hair and a sleeveless blouse stood back holding her stick.

"It's you, girl," the black guy said stepping back.

There were probably twenty people milling around in back by the tables. A few were obviously drunk. One girl was asleep or passed out at the back table. Books and journals lay all along the tables amongst ashtrays, coffee and soft-drink containers. Everybody was talking a mile a minute, a couple people sat there, legs crossed, flat stoned, not moving a muscle. I had never seen an array of people like this before. The Beats of Venice! I was finally here.

I walked up to the counter and ordered two coffees. A young man with a blond beard wearing a corduroy jacket and sandals stepped up behind me. A plain-looking girl with long, straight hair stood beside him.

"Are you really going to be in that play?" she asked. "And Peter's directing it! I can't believe it, I am so jealous."

"Yes, darling, and Jan Sterling will be coming down to be in it. I'm so excited I think my heart might pop right out of my body."

I looked back at him. A faggot, I thought.

Jeff had disappeared by the time I got back outside. I stood looking around for him. No Jeff. I set his coffee on a ledge by a window and stood there drinking mine.

"Your friend went out there to the parking lot, if that's who you're looking for."

I turned around to see a light-complexioned black man leaning against the building. He was about twenty-six or twenty-seven. I had seen him earlier out by the drum players. He had tight, curly hair and a thin-haired mustache, the teeth slightly bucked. He wore Levis and a Mexican poncho that hung below the waist. He was holding a beret in his left hand and a coffee cup filled with red wine in the other. "Oh that's where he went. I guess he'll get back when he gets back," I said, looking out over the parking lot.

The black man stood there looking at me, drinking out of his cup, then he smiled, "You're new around here aren't you? I don't recall seeing you before. My name is Dale."

"Yeah, I've only been here a few days. I've been on the road. I was here a couple of years ago. Don't know how I could have missed this area." I pulled out a cigarette and lit it. "They call me Pat. Are you living down here at the beach?"

"Yeah I've been here a couple of years. I run a coffee house down at the other end of the beach. It's called the 'Bandit's Hideout' and it's strictly after hours. We open at eleven every night till seven in the morning, seven days a week. It's right in the very heart of town on the beach. Come on down and I'll buy you a coffee."

"I'll do it," I said. "How do you like living at the beach?" I asked.

"That's a hell of a question. Let's just say that you'll never catch my black ass in Toledo again."

"Toledo, Ohio?" I asked. "Hell, I'm from Detroit. I left Ohio, about a year ago." We talked for another ten minutes then he said he had to go to work. "I'll be down for that coffee," I said.

Jeff still wasn't back so I walked up the hill to the Venice North coffee shop to see what was happening.

I stepped through the door, the room was long and narrow with small square wooden tables. Three tables on each wall and three up the center; stained glass lamps sat on the tables. Two men with beards were playing an intense game of chess to my right. A girl about twenty, with dark hair pulled back in a pony tail, was sitting on the opposite side with her feet up on a second chair, reading a book. A man and women were leaning on a counter in back talking. One of the men at the chess game said, "Check."

As I walked toward the counter I glanced down to see what the girl was reading, "The Sane Society." Never heard of it! I ordered a coffee and went to sit down at the table next to the girl.

"Do you go to school around here?" I asked.

She looked up at me and held my eyes a second, "No," she said, and went back to her reading.

"Don't leave me in the dark, are we living in an insane society, or not?" I asked, taking a drink of coffee.

"Probably. Are you a cop?" She asked, still holding the book open.

"That's being a bit paranoid isn't it?" I said, pulling out a cigarette and lighting it. "Do I look like a cop with this long hair and goatee?"

She put the book face down on the table, "Look-it, Jack."

"Pat," I said.

"They come down here in bunches looking just like you, trying to pick up on a lone chick. You have to prove you're not a cop, at least to me, anyway."

"How, pray-tell, do I do that?" I asked, throwing my arms up into the air.

"Get a friend to vouch for you then I'll talk to you, otherwise don't fuck with me." She picked up her book and started reading again, as if we hadn't said a word. I drank the last of my coffee and stood up trying to think of something to say for the last word. The only thing I could think of was, Fuck this chick.

"You are rather cute though," she said, looking up, eyes sparkling.

I sat back down, hope growing in my heart and a smile on my face.

❧

Her name was Gina, and she came from Chicago. She told me her dad hated her being out here, living the bohemian lifestyle. He was a congressman back in Illinois, and thought a woman's place was in the home, taking care of a husband and a bunch of kids.

"I don't think he even thinks of me as a real person, just someone to make him look good. I couldn't stand it anymore. As soon as I was able, I got the hell out of there."

"So if you're not going to school, what are you doing out here a million miles away from home?" I asked.

"I'm painting. I won a scholarship to an art institute back east, and went there for nine months. It wasn't all that it was cracked up to be. I quit and came out here to live among people who are doing the thing." She folded the tip of a page in her book and closed it.

"Do I detect a slight accent?"

"I'm Russian, a Russian artist who is doing marvelous work in Venice Beach, and if you're a good boy I might show you some of my work sometime."

I looked into my empty cup then back at her, "I'm sick of coffee, how 'bout you and I going after a drink."

"Haven't you heard? The evening cocktail down here is a good joint. That's my choice," she said rolling her thumbs and forefinger together in imitation of rolling a joint.

"It just so happens I have a friend down below who should have scored by now. Let's take a walk down and see what he has," I said, standing up waiting for her.

She stood up, grabbing her jacket off the back of the chair and her book off the table. "Why not, I'd like a good smoke." We headed for the door. The chess players were still concentrating on their game, I nodded to the one that looked up.

☙

Gina and I walked down the hill in the gathering fog. I looked through the windows of the pizza house trying to spot Jeff. Several people were milling around the doorway. I spotted Jeff over by the parking lot talking to a couple of guys. I yelled and waved.

"Let's go sit on the wall," Gina said.

We walked over to the picnic shelter and sat on the wall listening to the musicians playing their drums and guitars.

Two blacks and a white guy were sitting on the back wall sharing a bottle of white port and laughing like they had their own private joke. Three people sat on a picnic table, the rest stood around moving to the music. I could see a joint being passed around in the crowd. The bottle of burgundy had found a friend; there were now two bottles sitting on the table.

Jeff came up and said, "Where ya been man, I've been look'in all over for ya." He grabbed my hand and put a small roll of tinfoil in it.

"Gina, Right?" he said, looking at Gina. She nodded her head up and down.

"I'm Jeff, Kate's brother. I met you a couple of weeks ago at her house. Ya remember me?" Gina nodded again,

"How is she doing? Slowing down a little, I hope." Gina said.

"Well she slept for a whole week, coming off that speed. She got a little strung out there for a while, but she's back among the living and gaining weight," Jeff said.

"How did you meet Pat here? This guy must be a pretty quick worker. I turn my back for a minute and he's picked up one of the best looking women on the beach."

Gina smiled, "I let him entice me down here with a promise, that a friend would have some weed."

"And that I have, lovely lady," Jeff said, pulling out a joint with two fingers and holding it straight up. "I'll let you do the honors."

"What's this?" I asked, unrolling the tinfoil.

"They're cross-tops, that's all I could get. Take a couple and see how you do. You can always take another."

Gina lit the joint and inhaled deeply, passing it over to Jeff.

I threw two bennies into my mouth and swallowed; they got stuck in my throat. I jumped off the wall and grabbed a bottle of wine to wash them down with.

"Man, did that taste like shit? I wonder what hell they're made of."

"Benzedrine," Jeff said.

"Touché, Gina. You want one?" I held out the roll for her to take.

"What did you have to pay for these?" I asked Jeff.

Gina took three and tossed them into her mouth, picking up the wine for a chaser.

"A buck a roll, there are ten to the roll," he said handing me the joint.

"Not a bad deal." I took a hit off the joint.

We sat there listening and swaying to the music; the flute playing ups and downs loudly, the drums lowly in the background, then the drums slowly beating louder. Suddenly Gina jump off the wall and started moving to the beat of the drums, answering some primal urge. The drums beat louder and faster, the flute keeping up in the background. Hips swaying, arms in the air, her hair no longer in a pony tail, but flying wildly about her head. She was a wild, exotic, lovely animal at that moment. The music coming up to a very loud crescendo, then everyone stopped, dead silence. The drums started slowly, then faster and faster. Gina kept up with the beat. For a while that's all there was, the beat in ever fiber of my being. Then all was silence, and people laughing and clapping. For a moment I sat there stunned at the silence, I jumped off the wall and started clapping with the rest.

Gina came over, out of breath and smiling. I threw my arms around her saying, "That was some of the best dancing I've ever seen. Where did you learn to do that?"

"Nowhere, I've been practicing on letting go of my inhibitions, just letting the body do what it wants, when it wants. It makes for a happier body."

"Hell, I have a problem with just regular dancing. I need a six-pack to get out on the floor," I said.

"One of the things about living at the beach, the longer you're here, the fewer inhibitions you have. There's such a variety of people around here; like winos, pimps, whores, beatniks, which include the artist, writer and poets, and all the wannabes. You have the gay crowd, the lesbians, the hardcore drug users, and the one thing that ties them all together are the drugs and alcohol. Then underlying all this are the cops. They go undercover and pop up almost anyplace, even in your bed fucking you."

"Sounds exciting as hell," Jeff said.

"Sure does," I said. "At some point I'd like to be a writer, but I need more life experience, what better place to get it then here."

"Believe me, if you hang around here you'll get your life experience, but whether you write it down is another thing," Gina said.

People were still hanging around the musicians. Others were sitting on the tables and the wall, drinking wine and smoking pot.

"There's a bar down the beach a ways. Let's go there and have a beer before they close," Jeff said.

"Sounds good to me, I met a guy a little while ago who runs a coffee shop down the other end of the beach. Said he's buying the coffee if we show up. How 'bout it, Gina, would you like to go?" I asked, sliding off the wall.

"Hell, yes, I was thinking of heading down to Bandits later anyway. Let's just say goodbye to Timba."

She walked over and put her arms around the big black guy that had been playing the conga drums.

"Hey, Pat, come on over here and meet Timba," she called.

Jeff and I walked over and said hello to the big guy. He had a Jamaican accent with a large booming voice.

He's probably from New York, I thought.

"How you doing, man," he said. "I want you should take care my little Gina." He looked me straight in the eye then gave me a big smile. "You smoke," he said, handing me the roach he had been smoking. "You good boy, I can tell."

It seemed that in Venice when you meet a person or leave a place, you have to take a few hits off a joint.

I took a hit and passed it to Jeff.

"You play a hell of a conga drum," I said.

"Thanks, I been playing for years now. I got out of jail yesterday. Big celebration today, man."

"Yeah, I know how that feels. We're going down to get a beer before the bar closes, so we'll catch you later, man." I said, feeling a little possessive of Gina, like he wanted to talk to her some more. Another day for that, I thought.

"Later," he said, eyeing me.

Jeff, Gina, and I started walking down the front, into the fog.

As we walked through the foggy night, my mind seemed to slow way down, while another part of me was speeding up. I was listening to Gina and Jeff talking about her painting, the colors, the brush strokes, the eyes of a schizophrenic. Up ahead three figures came into view; I had a touch of fear for a second, they seemed to be on horseback. Off to my right was a lone, shadowy figure walking on the beach. He too looked larger then life. The waves were slapping up on the shore, but the sound was so clear I could feel each wave hit through my body. Awareness, I thought, a new awareness.

The sign over the door was blinking on and off in red, The Sand Box. Three men with beards and long hair passed by, as we entered the bar. They wore dark clothes and sandals. Engrossed in conversation, I don't think they even saw us, or if they did, they didn't let on.

Beatniks ran through my mind. They were beautiful walking down the beachfront like that, trying to solve the world's problems. The various colored lights felt sensual as we walked into the small bar. Everything was wonderful, I had this feeling of love for every living thing.

Three large women with short haircuts sat at the bar; there were only five stools. They looked as if they could have been truck drivers. Four women were dancing as couples off the bar. Five tables circled around the perimeter.

"What a small place," Jeff said, and walked over to the bar.

Gina and I went to a table in the corner and sat down. There was a big picture window in the front wall with bamboo shades. The shades were three quarters of the way down.

"Kerouac," I said.

Gina looked at me, while sitting down at a small table.

"Jack Kerouac! I was just wondering if he could be in the area. Last week I read 'Howl' by Ginsburg. Have you read it? It blew my mind. Anyway, I just saw those beats outside and thought of him." I said, sitting down, looking around the room.

She shook her head no, "But, I met Ginsburg up in North Beach once for about two minutes in a coffee shop. He was a friend of a friend. At the time I'd never heard of him, but I've been meaning to read some of his work. Kerouac was here about six months ago. Timba told me, they ran through the sewers of Venice playing bongos at all the street intersections. By the time anybody figured out where they were, they were gone to the next one. Kerouac was only here a day and off he went. He's gotten too popular to hang out long," she said.

Jeff set a beer down in front of Gina, then put the other two on the table and sat down, "I think we've wandered into a lesbian bar," he said.

"It is! I thought you knew that when we came in," Gina said.

"No I didn't, I just knew there was a bar here. I'd never been in here before. I don't think I want to be hanging out with a bunch of lesbians," he said.

"You're not hanging with them, you're with us," I said, picking up my glass and taking a drink. The beer hit the veins under my tongue and sent a sensation all through my body. "Wow" I said, "was that different."

"There's a bunch of freaks in this bar man. Where in hell have you brought me?" a loud voice said.

I looked over at the door. Two men stood inside the door, four feet from the women seated at the bar. The men wore short sleeve shirts and slacks and marine style haircuts. The one nearest me stepped up behind the women and said something low.

The center woman swung around quickly and punched the first man right between the eyes. At the same instant the other two women swung around in opposite directions with beer mug in hand. The first guy took the mug in the temple, the second one took it alongside his jaw. The men were taken totally by surprise. The first one dropped to the floor on his knees. He sat back on his heels and shook his head. The second guy staggered back toward the door, but the big gal was all over him, arms whaling. The other two took heart, and one kicked the kneeling man in the chest. Then they both jumped on him.

"Ohhhhhh! Did I feel that," I said.

The second fellow sprang for the door screaming obscenities. The other two gals were beating hell out of first guy, then they reached down together and picked him up and threw him through the bamboo shades. The table went flying and we had to jump up and move quickly away. I grabbed my mug. The glass from the window flew everywhere. The guy and bamboo shades ended up on the walkway out front.

"So much for that beer," I said, setting it on a table that was still standing and stepped over to the window and looked out at the fellow who had been so belligerent, just a minute ago. He lay there bleeding, a big gash on the cheekbone. His friend was still screaming; at a fifty-foot distance from the door.

"Come on Jeff, let's see if we can give this guy a hand," I said, walking toward the door.

The women stood over their prey.

"All right ladies, you've proved your point. Now he needs to see a doctor."

"Fuck you, asshole. You want some of what he got?" one of the women said menacingly. They were all the same size, big.

"Cool your heels. You almost killed this poor bastard. Go have a beer and we'll see if we can get him to a hospital," I said, kneeling down by the injured man and looking at the other guy pacing in a semicircle.

The women still acted tough, and grumbled as they backed into the bar and disappeared.

"Hey, buddy. You guys got a car?" I asked.

The young man stood there with a bloody nose, torn shirt, grinding his fist into the palm of his hand. Fear seemed to dance around him like a lover.

"Yeah, sure, it's about a block over," he said, stepping back, then ahead, then back again.

"Well, go get it, and we'll meet you at the alley with your friend," I said.

He stopped and stood there a second wondering if he should trust us.

"OK," he said, turning and running off.

❧

Jeff and I walked back into the light of the boardwalk. Gina sat in the sand at the edge of the walk smoking a cigarette and drinking a beer. She looked up, smiling, "Well you've done your good deed for the day, now its beer time." She held up two bottles for us. "I got these just before they turned off the lights and closed the place down. They left rather quickly, I think," she said.

"I can't say I blame them, but I sure am glad you thought to get some beer. Let's go out on the beach and drink a few," I said, taking the beer and picking up the bag of bottles and heading out. Gina got up and followed along with Jeff.

I found a place by the shore and plopped down. The waves rolling up on the beach, more sound then sight. Through the fog I watched whitewater descend back into the ocean as if pulled by a magnet. A fog horn some distance off moaned forlornly.

"I learned something tonight," Jeff said. "Don't fuck with lesbians, man! Did you see that guy's face? The skin came right off the cheek bone and hung there. He's going to have one hell of a scar." Jeff fell down beside Gina.

Gina sat in the center opening a beer for herself.

"For a girl who doesn't like beer, you sure put it away," I said.

"I never said I didn't like beer. I just don't like being drunk most of the time," she said, putting the bottle to her lips and taking a drink. "Besides my painting goes to hell if I drink and I'm sick half the time. Smoking pot just mellows me out and I'm able to think in a more creative way. My painting seems to flow from an inner part of my being. I used to drink a lot back in Chicago. You know, the misunderstood artist. Now I try not to drink so often, but that doesn't mean I don't know how."

"Consider me put in my place," I said, leaning back on one elbow and pushing sand into little mounds with the bottle.

"And as for that guy who got thrown through the window, he got what he deserved. Maybe a little more then he deserved, but these square-minded people that come down here to the beach to look at the freaks need a lesson. It was just his turn that's all. I don't have any pity for him," Gina said, sitting there daring either of us to challenge her.

"All I'm saying is he got cut up pretty bad. I'm not taking sides," Jeff said. "I was just glad it wasn't me for Christ sake." He started rolling a joint.

"You're a cold-hearted woman, girl," I said. "If three men had been beating that guy I might have stepped in; but I was on the women's side, right till they threw his ass through the window. Then I realized these broads were really serious. I'm not sure how I feel about that," I said, taking a Pall Mall from my pack and passing the pack over to

Gina. "Want one?" I asked.

She took one and passed the pack back.

Flame lit up as Jeff struck his match to light the joint. I watched the flame as he held it for a minute after the joint was lit.

"Well," Gina said, "After you've lived here a while you'll understand. When you live here you're on the in. When you don't, you're a tourist, and tourists have to pay one way or the other. Some of these bastards are really sick and some are just naïve. Most come down here to appease their perverted ways. As far as the lesbians are concerned, I know those three women. One is a little odd, but the other two are decent. They mind their own business. They don't have to take shit off every sicko that walks into the bar."

She took the joint from Jeff's offered hand.

We sat there in silence. My mind going everywhere at once and nowhere. I felt like we'd been there for hours. "I'm on your side girl, How long we been sitting here anyway? It feels like hours."

"Just a few minutes; it's the pot," she said.

Jeff started laughing and rolling around in the sand, "Man, I'm high as hell. I think we should start moving or my whole body may explode." He stood up and started walking.

"Let's head for Bandits, it's that time of night," Gina said, getting up.

☙

Back on the boardwalk we trudged our way south, heading for the all-night coffee house. I felt as though we walked in a blue haze bubble, all safe and secure. The fog that enveloped us was thick and damp, but I didn't notice it; I was feeling this strange kind of love for the whole planet. For a moment there, and it only lasted ten seconds, I felt like I understood the universe. Then it was gone and I was left with this magnificent wonder.

"WOW! What a rush, man. I think I experienced a type of nirvana," I said, as I moved over to a bench and sat down to think about it.

"Yeah, man, it's the dope. This is some goo-ood stuff," Jeff said, as if he was feeling the same thing. He opened a beer and took a drink.

"Crack me one of those, will ya, my mouth feels like a cottonball," I said.

Jeff paced in front of me and Gina danced around on her tip toes. I felt around in my pocket and found the tin foil holding the cross tops. There were three left, we each took one.

"Well, we're out of beer and dope. So we'll have to pick up some more,"

Gina said. "I for one am ready to move on, and go see the wizard."

"I second that," I said, getting up and grabbing Gina and Jeff around the shoulders. She lifted a leg and started to step forward, Jeff and I followed her lead, singing, "We're off to see the wizard, the wonderful Wizard of Oz." We marched down the boardwalk.

✑

We had meandered our way up the beach and through the dark alleys of Venice, talking all the way. I thought I'd been saying some of the most profound things, but looking back at it I was just motor-mouthing. The speed was working.

We stepped out of an alley onto the Boulevard. "This is it," Gina said.

We were only a couple of hundred yards from the beach. I was looking at a one-story black building, no windows, a small white light hung over the door, illuminating a small area in the alley. Across the alley was a three-story, fading white apartment building that looked like it had been built at the turn of the century. On the south side of the street was a large field. East of the field was a parking lot half full with cars. The bar next to it was just closing for the night. Fifteen or twenty people came out the door talking and singing and went to their various cars.

A red light was over the main entrance and a small sign saying, 'The Bandits Hideaway' hung over the door, almost invisible. I let Gina walk in first, then I followed, Jeff bringing up the rear. The room appeared to be almost dark. The walls were painted black and the only white lights were the florescence lights over the two pool tables off to my left. Large colored lights hung from the ceiling's edge, spaced every fifteen feet. A bar ran from front to back with twenty captains chairs, over half were filled with an assortment of weird looking people. A four-foot high wall, five feet off the bar, ran almost the length of the room, open at either end. The pool tables were on the other side. In the corner to my left sat a large waterfall that had seen better days; there was no water to fall. Small groups of people stood around talking. Jazz flowed from speakers in the ceiling permeating the atmosphere; you couldn't help but feel the groove.

Gina slid between two men talking and made her way over to the waterfall and sat down on it, I was right behind her. Jeff tapped me on the shoulder and said, "I'll grab us some coffee." I nodded my head in the affirmative and sat down beside Gina.

"Man, this is great," I said, watching all the people. Most of the white men wore long hair and beards of one form or another, with baggy clothes. A few black men sported afros, but most wore trim suits with thin ties and small rimmed hats with colored bands. They tried to look like pimps. The pool tables were hot, balls were hitting pockets quicker then I could count. Bets were being laid down, pretty good money too.

Jeff showed up with the coffee. I sat watching, my mind going a mile a minute. After a long period it seemed I stood up and told the others I'd be back in a few minutes, I was going over to say hello to Dale at the bar. "Just a minute," Jeff said. He handed me two little red capsules, and said, "Take these, they will counteract the speed and keep you mellow." I tossed them down my throat, chased with some coffee and headed for the bar.

Dale was no where in sight. Instead, a tall, black kid with short-shorts was behind the bar. His shirt tied up around his rib cage and the tail hung over his buttocks, a ring in one ear. He was sashaying back and forth, lips pursed, head held high. A swinging faggot if ever I seen one, I thought.

"And what would you like you dear, sweet man?" And there he was right in front of me. "Dale," I said "I'm looking for Dale."

"Ah shucks! And I thought you were looking for me, I'm prettier than him."

"And that you are, but he's the one I'm looking for."

"He's in the back room making sandwiches. I'm the star of this show. When you're done doing him come do me I'll show you a good time." He showed me his big white teeth. I laughed, trying to think of something to say, then said the hell with it, and went to the back room.

❧

The back room was small, ten by twelve. A large coffee urn sat on a table to my right, a double cast iron sink hung on the back wall, a table in be-tween. To my left a single-wide mattress lay on the floor. Dale stood behind the table wrapping sandwiches in cellophane.

"Hey! My man, what's happening?" I said from the doorway.

Dale looked up and gave me a smile, "Pat, right? From the pizza house. Give me a minute while I take these sandwiches out to Walton." He picked up the tray and walked out the door. He was back in less than a minute.

I leaned up against the door jam. "So, how long you been running this place?" I asked.

He started pouring coffee grounds into a stainless steel container.

"About eight months. Scottie asked me to run it after the last guy got busted for selling weed. It's not a bad gig. I get to know a lot of people, besides I haven't the slightest idea what I want to do with myself. This place gives me the thinking time I need."

"Did you take up where the other guy left off?" I asked. He looked at me.

"You know selling the weed." I said, taking a smoke out of my pocket and lighting it.

"Hell, no, I ain't ready to spend that much time in jail. Besides there are a hell of a lot of guys ready to sell dope out there, I don't have to."

He reached over and grabbed a pitcher of water sitting on the table, and poured it into the coffee urn. "Scottie is a small-time gangster, or he thinks he is. He just wants somebody to run the place. If you sell dope, that's your thing. He'll try and get you out of jail if he can. He has a friend who runs a bail bonds office downtown. The asshole even tries to sell babies on the black market."

"Come on, man, babies, how in hell can a guy sell babies?"

"There are hundreds of couples out there jumping through hoops every day trying to get a kid; and most often they don't succeed. That's where guys like Scottie come in. He's only sold one that I know of. His girlfriend had a kid a while back and they sold her. Made a pretty good bundle on that one, I guess, enough that he's trying to break into the business now."

He pulled the top over to close the lid, and flipped the switch on. "We're outta here."

As we came back into the main room I looked around for Gina and Jeff. I couldn't see them for all the people standing. As I stood looking around, Gina's head appeared in the sea of people, and she started walking toward the bar. I came up at the other end, hoping to get her attention. She had gotten to the bar and was trying to get Walton's attention. She didn't see me.

Two black men slid in beside her on the left, forcing her to move down the bar a little. It didn't seem to upset her; she kept trying to get the bartender's attention. Another black man moved in on her right. From where I stood at the other end of the bar I could see two more men behind her. I was just starting to move in that direction, when one of the men put his arm out in front of her and pushed her back into the men behind. He moved into her spot.

I stood watching, not believing what I saw. My brain wouldn't connect to my eyes. But all the time my mind knew what was going down. The three men in front made an about face, and the whole herd started shuffling toward the door. Gina became invisible.

My brain finally made contact with the eyes, then my hands, as I pushed away from the bar. I got the lead out of my feet and started shouldering my way through people to get to the front, yelling as I went, "They got Gina! Stop them." I couldn't seem to get moving, everybody was blocking the way. I felt they were doing it on purpose, and started pushing harder. I heard someone behind say, "Som bitch." I kept going forward. Finally I got to the front of the room and yelled over in Jeff's direction, I couldn't see him but hoped he was there,

"Jeff! Jeff, they got Gina!"

The noise of people, music, and my own internal yelling was loud in my ears as I burst through the door out onto the sidewalk.

My foot slipped six inches on the wet pavement as I came to a stop. All of a sudden everything was quiet in the still of early morning. The lights were dim in the heavy fog. A big dark Chevy sat at the curb idling peacefully. The muted grunts of the struggle before me were the only sounds on the street. Two men were laboring their burden into the back seat of the big car. "Come on, get the bitch in." I heard someone say from inside the car.

I stepped forward with a primal yell that even startled me and grabbed the first guy, throwing him toward the rear of the car. I reached for Gina's arm at the same time kicking the other guy in the hip, knocking him to one knee. There was a guy in the back seat that I hadn't noticed; he had a hold on Gina's hair and kept yelling to the driver, "Take off, George! Take off, will ya!" The thought ran through my head that I was going to lose her; then it happened, an ear-banging shot stopped everything. I looked up and over the car and Dale stood there with a pistol in his left hand looking at the driver. He must have come out the side door.

"Now that I have your attention, he said, what the hell you niggers doing down here trying to steal a woman out of my place? Don't you know I'm going to shoot your balls off if you don't turn the girl loose."

The guy in the back seat let go of Gina's hair. The driver started yelling, "Hey, man! Take it easy. We don't want no trouble, we just want a little pussy, man. We'll let her go. We're not going to hurt her."

I pulled Gina out and stood up. "You OK?" I asked.

Jeff was holding the man down with his knee, his fist in mid-swing. He was looking through the window of the car wondering if he just got shot. The big guy at the rear of the car stood whimpering, holding his shoulder. A knife lay at his feet. Walton with his short shorts and tennies was waltzing around him swinging a baseball bat, "Come on, mother-fuckers, I want to crack some more skulls."

"I'm OK. I can't believe those fuckers did that," she said.

Dale was on the other side of the car looking in through the window at the driver; I could see the gun pressed lightly to his head, "Shove those two in the back seat, Pat," he said to me. I grabbed the guy with the bum shoulder and pushed him toward the car. Jeff pulled up on the other one and pushed him into the back seat.

"Now I want you fellows to get your black asses out of here quick before the heat shows up. It's going to take me a week to explain all this shit. Don't let me see your face's around here for a while," Dale said.

The big Chevy, with its engine roaring and tires screaming, sped off into the dark fog.

We all stood there looking at one another for a moment, then Dale said, "All right, everybody inside. The cops'll be here any minute." He disappeared around the side of the building.

I reached for Gina and hugged her to me. Jeff, bringing up the rear, grabbed her around the waist and pulled her back to him. "I'm sure glad we didn't lose you, baby," he said, patting her head like a puppy. We walked back inside.

People stood around talking and shaking their heads, milling around the front door. Walton was dancing around, shooing everyone back inside, "People, listen up. It's time to move inside. The heat will arrive at any moment now and I don't want to be standing out here on the sidewalk with my bare-assed legs when they pull up." He was still waving the baseball bat around in the air when we went through the door.

Once we got inside I led Gina over to the waterfall and sat down, with Jeff right behind us. "Are you sure you're OK?" I asked, "I can take you home if you want." Most everybody was back where they were before the ruckus started. Walton had put the baseball bat away and was wiping down the counter with a self-satisfied look on his face. The music had stopped and you could hear the billiard balls bouncing off each other. People started talking in low tones, as if in anticipation for the final act to happen. Dale was nowhere in sight. The Man was coming and we all knew it, so if you were holding anything that you didn't want the man to see, now was the time to get rid of it.

Miles Davis' "Sketches of Spain" started in the background. "Yeah, I'm all right, I just want to sit here for a while. Besides the cops will just roust us if we try walking out of here," Gina said, pulling her hair back into a pony tail and putting a rubber band on it. She looked so cool sitting there I couldn't believe it. In my eyes she looked prefect, like she just left the theater and was about to have dinner. Jeff set the coffee on the table and sat down next to Gina. "You look good, everything's going to be all right." He crossed his legs and leaned back against the wall, sipping his coffee.

I looked up and saw a cop come in the side door. He stood there, watching. Three cops came in the front door. One of them walked over to the counter and started talking to Walton, who shook his head and talked with his arms. Finely he reached down and turned on the bright lights. Everybody acted as if they were going blind, putting their hands over their eyes and complaining about the light. The cops moved through the crowd talking to a few people here and there. There was a commotion at the bar. One guy was getting frisked as a cop walked up to us. "You hear any shots or anybody getting shot at?"

I shook my head, no, and said, "Been sitting right here and didn't hear a thing." I should have kept my mouth shut.

"OK, on your feet, put everything in your pockets on the table," he rubbed all over my body and in the waist band. "Go ahead and sit down," he said, and moved on to another group. The cops were there another ten minutes and took one guy with them when they left.

"Well, that's over," I said, leaning back and putting the back of my hand to my forehead feigning relief. I sat back up and said, "I think it's time to exit this place, don't you, my friends?" Gina nodded and Jeff started to get up. "Wait" I said, "I'll be right back. I have to say thanks to Dale. Without his six shooter, we'd had a hell of a lot more difficulty." I headed to the back and Gina followed.

Dale was standing at the end of the bar with one foot up on a stool talking to Walton.

"Hey Walton, I want to tell you that was one of the best baseball swings I ever seen. That guy will be trying to get his arm back in place next Tuesday," I said, as we came up and leaned on the bar next to Dale.

Walton lifted his right hand up by his cheek and with a limp wrist, pointed a finger at me. "For you, my pretty one, I would go to the end," he said, sticking his hip out and giving Gina a wink of the eye. Then he turned and sashayed down to the other end of the bar.

I looked over at Dale and said, "I owe you big time. Those guys would have stomped my ass if you hadn't been there."

"Me too, it was my butt that almost got hauled away," Gina said. I'm really moved to tell you how much I appreciate it." Gina grabbed Dale's hand and give it a squeeze.

"No thanks necessary. It just goes along with the service," Dale said, showing his big white teeth through the smile.

"My ass, you could have got yourself all jammed up over that situation. Anyway, enough said. I'm going to walk Gina home and I'll be seeing you here tomorrow night or maybe on the beach, whatever comes first." I turned to go, then turned back, "Oh, by the way, what did you do with that gun? The cops didn't get it."

He gave me another of his smiles and said, "It was in a drain pipe down the street."

"Later, man," I said, getting in behind Gina and following her toward the door.

Out on the street Jeff was nowhere in sight. I stepped back inside to look around and there he was over on the far wall talking to a tan chick; she was a real beauty. Gina came up behind me. "Don't leave me alone out there," she said, pulling on my chalecko.

"Oh, shit baby I'm sorry," I said, turning to look at her then putting my arm around her. "I had my head somewhere else."

We walked over to the table "What's happening?" I asked, looking down at the girl. I almost got jealous. She had caramel colored skin, thin lips, and a straight nose with smoky, dark eyes. Her black hair bunched up behind her head, with long curls hanging down.

Jeff looked up at me, "Oh, this is Dana. Dana this is Pat, a friend of mind from down Texas way. We used to fish down on the Gulf of Mexico." She looked up at me with a half-smile and slowly lifted her right hand for me to take.

I took her hand and held it. She's loaded, I thought, but what the hell, so am I. "How you doing, Dana. It's great to know ya. This here is Gina."

"We know each other! How is it, Dana. You look like you got some good stuff," Gina said.

With half-closed eyes Dana smiled. "Ya for sure, some good stuff."

"Dana and I are old friends," Jeff said, "I thought as long as you were going to take Gina home, I'd hang out with Dana and make sure she got home OK. How's that with you?" Jeff looked at me and smiled.

I couldn't believe my luck. "Hey man, sounds good to me. I'll catch up with you tomorrow then." I turned to go then looked back, "Nice to meet ya Dana, talk at ya later."

Gina reached over and rubbed Jeff's arm, squeezing it a little, "Thanks Jeff, I appreciate what you did tonight. We'll see you later then. Stay cool," and out the door we went.

ℰↄ

Gina and I rounded the corner and walked down the boardwalk. "How you feeling about walking down here? We could take a taxi if you want," I said, putting my arm around her and bringing her in close to me.

"Hell, no, I'm not going to let a few bullies scare me off the beach," she said, pulling away from me and pushing her hands down deeper into the pockets of her jacket. "I'm not going to become a fearful, helpless, woman, over this shit. It's something like being thrown from a horse; if I don't walk this beach tonight I'll always have a little fear of it. Besides, you're here with me," Gina smiled up at me.

We walked along in silence for a while, her in that defiant mood, and me wondering how to act. Then she moved in close and slipped her arm under mine. It was like a message from heaven. My mind cleared and I felt in control again.

"With all that we drank tonight I'm amazed how clear my mind is. I feel like I could go on for another night," I said, lifting my arms and twirling around.

"Well, considering all that's happened, I don't feel too bad myself," she said, grabbing my arm back. We walked along the boardwalk as if in a bubble of our own. The early morning fog engulfed us. We had about ten feet visibility, the rest of the world seemed surreal.

Gina nudged me to the right and we turned up a street stopping at a brown two-storied brick apartment building with a lower unit and an upper unit. Both doors faced the street. Gina opened the door on the west side of the building and started up the stairs, and I followed her in. The walls were freshly painted, an off white. Three paintings were hung along the staircase, each were two and a half feet square. Each painting had its own illuminating light over it. As I walked up the stairs I looked at the first painting, it was an abstract. I couldn't grasp anything from it. I moved to the next as if I was some sort of art critic. I didn't know a thing about art. In fact Gina was the only artist I'd ever met. This painting was in greens, blues, and whites. The images were the busts of three figures, side by side in profile, all three were green. The profile lines were straight. What stopped me were the eyes. They looked back at me. I stood there looking at the painting and became engrossed in it. The eyes on the second profile I'd swear I'd seen before, maybe in the mirror. Gina had went on ahead up the stairs and was moving around up there.

"Is this fellow in the center your schizophrenic?" I yelled up the stairs, knowing the answer.

"Yes," she said, as her head popped out from around the corner. "How do you like it?"

"I think they're great," I said, moving up to the next painting. This one was a harbor scene with sailboats and fishing boats in the background on a quiet, foggy morning. I continued up to the top of the stairs and stepped into a large room. A kitchen was off to the left. A twin-size mattress lay on the floor next to the wall. A table six inch's high had been placed by the mattress. It held half empty tubes of paint and drawing pencils. Art books and magazines were strung out around the end of the mattress. The walls were covered with drawings, all kind's, there were nudes, drawings of old men playing checkers, old women selling fruit, people walking the boardwalk. Three big pillows were on the floor up against the opposite wall. Two large windows on the east wall, an easel sat in the middle of the room with a gray canvas sitting on it. The room looked well lived in.

"Do you like tea?" Gina asked, reaching for two cups hanging under the cupboard.

"Sure," I said. I moved over to the wall and started looking at the drawings.

"Man, you're really good. I'm impressed," I said, pulling a smoke out of my pocket. I don't know if it was the speed I'd eaten or what, but each picture had a significance that caught me and held me captive. It was a full twenty minutes before I turned around to find Gina sitting on the mattress Indian-style quietly drinking her tea, watching me over the rim of her cup.

"Your tea is here on the table. It's almost cold. Come over here and sit down," Gina said, patting the mattress next to her.

I plopped down beside her, picked up the tea and tasted it. My mouth felt like I'd been chewing on cotton. I held the tea in my mouth for a minute, then swallowed. That's when I noticed the Buddha statue sitting on the floor opposite us, up against the wall between two pillows.

"I'm what they call half-assed good. I've got a lot to learn. I'm thinking of going back to school, but I want to get a few more things done to be able to show," she said, taking a drink of her tea.

"Girl, I just wish I had half your talent," I said, leaning over and lifting her chin up kissing her full on the mouth, Gina responded by putting her hand on the back of my head and pressing forward, then pulling away.

"Do you mind terribly if we don't have sex right now. I want you to lie with me and hold me for a while. Is that OK?" she asked, looking up at me, rubbing my forearm.

"I can do that," I said, kissing her lightly, and wishing that the erection that had appeared so suddenly would go away.

"What's with the Buddha?" I asked, trying to change the subject. "Are you a Buddhist?"

"No," she laughed, "I hardly know anything. I read a book by Allen Watts, and liked the philosophy. It's about being here now, accepting this moment in time, being aware of the now. She stood up and went over and pushed a button. The lights went out and I sat there in the semi-darkness of the predawn. Gina came back and stood before me taking off her blouse and pants, leaving the bra and panties on, then she lay down beside me.

"You can bet that beautiful ass of yours that I'm aware of the now," I said, reaching out rubbing the small of her back. I took my shirt off and kicked off the shoes. I didn't trust myself to take off the pants, and lay down beside her. Gina came into my arms and snuggled her face into my chest. I lay like that for a long time feeling her warmth and rubbing her back every once in a while, but sleep would not come. I lay there in a kind of semi-sleep, not sleeping, not awake, just being there, thinking I could get up anytime. Dawn appeared and still I lay there holding this girl, trying to make it last, but alas my mind got the better of me and I had to get up and take a walk. My arm was asleep and I had to keep bending it to get it working again. I pulled on my shoes and leaned over and gave Gina a kiss on the temple and said, "I'll be back in a little bit I'm going for a walk."

She rolled over and her face disappeared under her hair. "I'll be here."

వ

It was a damp, foggy morning at the beach, but I'd bet that most mornings in Venice, California are like that. On the boardwalk, I looked in both directions, then saw a neon sign blinking on and off. I walked down there and got a cup of coffee to go and returned to the picnic area where the musicians had been playing the night before. I jumped up on the wall and sat there watching the ocean, drinking my coffee. I'd made it to the west coast and found it was all true, the possibilities were endless. I could sit down and write the Great American Novel maybe, or become an artist of some sort, learn to play the guitar. Thinking about the people I'd met in the last two days proved there was something happening here and I wanted to be part of it. I don't think I ever felt that before. It was as if I was on the verge of something great about to happen. I sat there, on the wall lost in my reverie, when a big, blond guy jumped up on the wall beside me. He had long hair and hadn't seen a razor in a couple of weeks, a green t-shirt and Levi's, but his feet were bare. He unscrewed the cap off a bottle of wine and lifted it toward me, "You want a taste?"

"No man, not today, I've got a lady waiting for me," I said, lifting my cup up in a salute.

"Suit yourself," he said, lifting the bottle to his lips.

I noticed a tattoo on the forearm, "What's that say on your arm?"

He turned his arm over so I could get a better look. "I think, therefore I am," I read it aloud. "What the hell does that mean?" I asked, looking at him as if he was nuts.

"That's a quote from Descartes, man. It means, I'm not a machine, I'm a person, and an artist. I put it on my arm so that the next time I go look for a job maybe I'll remember what's important, my art or the money, and hopefully it's not the money, man." He looked at me as if I knew what he was talking about. He took another drink from the bottle. "What do you do?" he asked.

"Me, I do nothing, I said. My life is an art form. I've been on the road for the past year. I got into town two days ago and I'm trying to figure my next move, hang out here for awhile, then head up to San Francisco to check out that scene." I said.

He nodded his head, in agreement. Maybe he knew what I was talking about, but I didn't have a clue.

I jumped off the wall and brushed my hands together, "Well, like I said, I've got a lady waiting. Talk at you later man."

He tipped the bottle toward me. "Later, man."

I started walking away then stopped, as an afterthought. "Hey, man, have you ever seen any little, purple, heart-shaped bennies around?"

℘ ℘ ℘